ATLANTASTAN

CHAOS CITY

CHRIS GREEN

URBAN AINT DEAD

CONTENTS

SOUNDTRACKS

Scan the QR Code below to listen to the Soundtracks/Singles of some of your favorite U.A.D titles:

Don't have Spotify or Apple Music?
No Sweat!
Visit your choice streaming platform and search URBAN AINT DEAD.

Currently on lock serving a bid?

JPay, iHeartRadio, WHATEVER!
We got you covered.

Simply log into your facility's kiosk or tablet, go to music and search
URBAN AINT DEAD.

URBAN AINT DEAD

Like & Follow us on social media:
FB - URBAN AINT DEAD
IG: @urbanaintdead
Tik Tok - @urbanaintdead

SUBMISSIONS

Submit the first three chapters of your completed manuscript to urbanaintdead@gmail.com, subject line: Your book's title. The manuscript must be in a .doc file and sent as an attachment. The document should be in Times New Roman, double-spaced, and in size 12 font. Also, provide your synopsis and full contact information. If sending multiple submissions, they must each be in a separate email. Have a story but no way to submit it electronically? You can still submit to URBAN AINT DEAD. Send in the first three chapters, written or typed, of your completed manuscript to:

URBAN AINT DEAD
P.O Box 448
Maybrook, NY 12543

DO NOT send original manuscript. Must be a duplicate.
Provide your synopsis and a cover letter containing your full contact information.
Thanks for considering URBAN AINT DEAD.

ACKNOWLEDGMENTS

I would like to thank the entire UAD publishing and my brother Elijah for this opportunity to continue with giving the readers my craft and mind. I enjoy writing and plotting the best stories that I can for our audience, and this is a career that I will pursue for the rest of my life. My time in confinement is now coming to an end and before it's over I have to show my gratitude to the ones that has stood beside me the most.

First, Allah, my beautiful and strong hearted wife K. Green, my mama Dolsellia, my aunt, sister, grandma, cousin Michelle, my daughter Cerenity. My twin De'Angelo, my uncle Kevin, and the rest of the green family. I would like to thank all of my brothers that has stood behind me in these walls of confinement. My little brother, Juntavious Burton(Tayway), Joseph Atkinson (N.O), James Byrd(Dogghead), Mecco Mckinney (Mecco), my brother Fadricius Pope(Freddie), Stanley Dixon (Swayy), Thaddeus Roberts (BG), Shatner Thomas (Munchie)...If your name was left out I genuinely forgot, or it wasn't meant to be placed in. No hard feelings..Enjoy this new story and the rest to come. UADfortheWin sir!

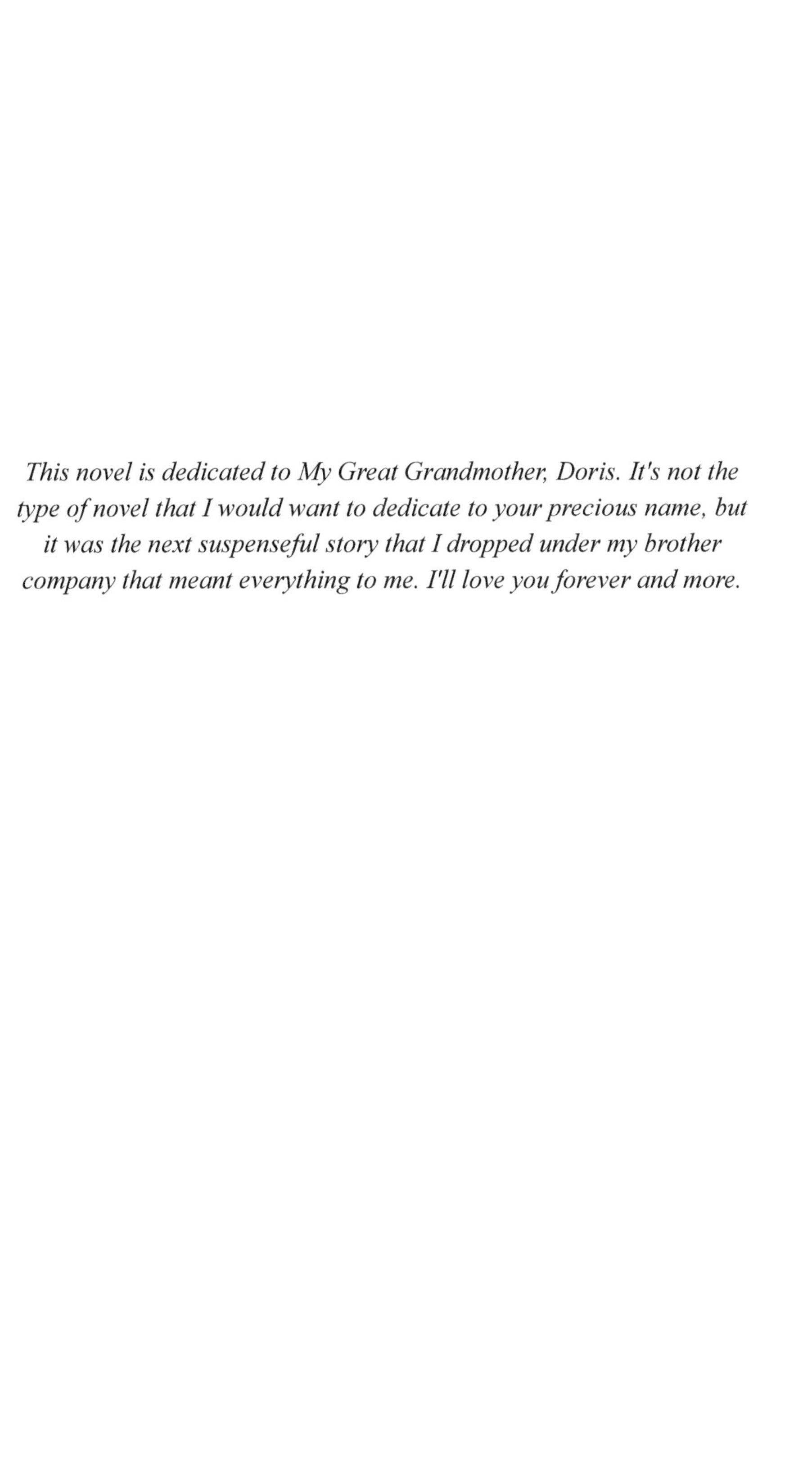

This novel is dedicated to My Great Grandmother, Doris. It's not the type of novel that I would want to dedicate to your precious name, but it was the next suspenseful story that I dropped under my brother company that meant everything to me. I'll love you forever and more.

PROLOGUE

(Unknown)
Club Lucky
Atlanta, GA (2026)
Cleveland Avenue

As my bodyguard cruised my 2024 AMG Benz down the streets of Atlanta, my mind was still pondering on my recent problem. The individual who constantly seemed to cause me anger and mixed emotions that I couldn't understand was picking at my skin like a razor nipping at the scab of a cut. Sometimes, I didn't know if it was just me in my feelings or if this bitch really had a spell on me. I was a person that demanded what I wanted. I had whatever I wanted. Portions of the city was at my grasp. I was more superior in my mind because I was the one who did the impossible. My heart was in an unstable place, and as the seconds ticked, my flesh tensed a bit.

"Tizo, pull over in the club. I'm ready," I ordered to my top assassin.

I never had to worry when Tizo was around because he always

showed up to handle the business and his job to perfection. As my car came to a halt, he parked directly in front of the entrance. Stepping out, he opened the back door, so I could rise from the backseat. My feet touched the ground, looking like nothing less than a million dollars. My respect was never a request; it was a demand. District 10, Zone 3 wasn't even my territory fully, but it damn sure felt like it.

I walked toward the entrance with my guard glued to my side. I moved past all the waiting guests, and the rope was removed before I could step close to the entrance. The music was beating like a migraine, and the strip joint was lit as usual. See, in Club Lucky, it held some of the baddest bitches out of Georgia, hoes that would make you triple take, fuck double. It was the year 2026 in Atlanta, and the murder rate was placed on a new ceiling when it came to organizations, hoods, families, and respect. After 2024, the murder rate was so high that the government renamed some areas by districts. It made it so that people were aware of the ones to stay out of at a certain time because after sunlight clicked down behind the clouds, even the police would be too scared to blare their sirens too loud.

Looking to my right, my eyes immediately locked in on the stripper that held the stage. She was finishing her song, and I only had my visual set for one bitch. Right as my mind went into think mode, the DJ started another song and introduced the next dancer to the stage.

"Aye, y'all know what fucking time it is. This goddess of the A, The Nigerian Queen that possesses all the sweeter things. I'm talking about the encore of the night. Give it up for the chocolate glass of milk herself, Riooooo!"

Hearing her name alone forced my fingers to reach for the 9mm pistol I had concealed. I scanned all the niggas and witnesses around me, making sure that if anyone looked like they had an irrational thought, it got placed back into their mind. Just when I thought she would never appear on the stage, I spotted her luscious legs swiping through the curtain, falling straight into a split. The noise boomed off the wall, and wads of cash were slung from every direction.

Rio jiggled her juicy ass like water, rising slowly back to her feet. Her body started to twerk and move, forcing the crowd to place all attention on her. I had to admit, she was nice. Long brown hair, Jamaican and Nigerian with a vixen body, and the fact that she was literally born with a silver spoon added to her ego. Her eyes were stardust gold, with pink lips, and the smile of a Maybelline model. Every nigga that was about something wanted her by their side, but she was already taken.

I watched her move for the next few minutes, and my heart still felt no different. Not a bit of compassion was moving through me. Regardless of how much I wanted to turn away, business was business. Nodding to Tizo, he pulled his lemon squeeze Glock 40 from his hip. Even through the loud blaring speakers, you could hear the gunshots roar from his pistol.

Boom! Boom! Boom! Boom! Boom!

I watched Rio fall face first, her head colliding with the first step on the stage. The club erupted in pandemonium. Guests ran for the exit, ducking for cover, and I pushed the thought of regret to the back of my mind as I turned around to leave. Tizo guided me safely back out to the car, opening the back door for me to climb inside. I knew that my actions would surely begin a war. I was in the race to secure every district in Atlanta and was already fifty percent at my goal. The only person that I knew would come for answers was the exact motherfucker I needed to place an end to… Rude Boy. I just knew it wouldn't be an easy task.

CHAPTER ONE

Rude Boy
Weston Hotel (Luxury Suite)

Pacing back and forth around the room, the tears couldn't stop pouring down my face, and it felt like the rage of a bull was trying to bust through my chest. I'd just received the call that my wife, Shanti, had been murdered on the premises of her job. The confusion of what took place had my mind doing somersaults. I knew that she was in that nigga, Polar's territory, District 10, but the codes of family, wives, and children were always off limits, regardless of time frame. Now that my wife's life had been taken, codes and rules were off. I wanted answers and bodies from whoever played a part in the treacherous stunt.

Pulling out my pistol, I shot three slugs through the wall in frustration.

Boom! Boom! Boom!

I didn't hesitate to kick the glass patio door, that was to my right side, to pieces before sitting down on the leather couch. My crew,

Daffy, Cinco, JoJo, and Bonnie, stood around quietly, watching me grieve, but no one said a word. My eyes shifted down to the squirming bodyguard that I had bound and gagged with a pillowcase over his head. I shot a brutal kick to his face before snatching it off, so the bitch nigga could look me in my eyes before he perished.

"Fuckkk, man, Rude, wha-what is this about, my nigga? I been loyal to you ever since you hired me, dawg. Goddamn, my nigga!" he uttered with blood pouring from his face.

"All y'all fuck niggas say the same thing when it's time to die." I stood over him, pointing my burner down toward his head. Squeezing the trigger three times, I opened up his brain with two and placed the last slug into the center of his chest.

Boom! Boom! Boom!

"Goddamn, Rude, you could of at least seen what the fuck he would spill first, man. How we gonna find out what happened to Rio if you slaughtering shit before we can ask the questions?" Daffy spoke up, turning his head away from the gruesome scene.

"Because the bitch nigga was gonna lie regardless, just like he did when I snatched the pillowcase off his head. I paid this bitch to be Shanti's bodyguard, so he's the first motherfucker that should know what happened to my lady," I spat through gritted teeth.

"Do you think the Kiss Squad got some'n to do with this?" Bonnie asked, raising her head.

"Right now, everybody is a suspect, but if my mind had to fucking guess, you damn right Polar would be the first on my list."

"So, what you want us to do cause you know we can blaze this shit up in every district until the snitches come telling? We will just have to deal with Lo on the back end, ya feel me?" Cinco added in.

I pondered in his response cause Lo was a hell of an asshole to deal with. The city was under his control and, not only that, he had power in every district. The city of Atlanta had done a major flip in the past few years, and the murder rate was up nearly eighty-five percent and still increasing by the tons due to new crews and leaders. Law enforcement was limited. It became so bad that the government issued a state of emergency. They gave every zone and surrounding county their own district and allowed people to govern the best they saw fit. The districts were controlled by the most ruthless criminals, and after sunset, if you were caught behind the territory of an enemy's district, your life was fair game. There was nothing a cop or law official could do about it.

All that flipped once Lo became the leader of district one, which was downtown Atlanta, the wealthiest and most secured zone in the city. He was like the God of the A and had his hands inside everything in the state. He was also the one that made wives, children, and families off limits. Those three things were sacred as long as the head of whatever district didn't violate a code of his rulebook, even after the territorial time limit. That bullshit was just broken when they allowed my woman to be slain while working in a place of business under his city, and I wanted equal blood back and some.

"Fuck Lo! We will deal with him how it comes, but until I get that call or a notice for a sit down, I'm cutting these bitches' throats the omerta way. If one of those Kiss Squad niggas is caught down bad our way, don't hesitate. Besides that, nothing else is to be shooken up without my permission."

"Understood." Daffy nodded before I made my way out of the hotel suite.

I sent a quick text for my cleanup crew to come and assist my team with the bodyguard's body, but at that moment, I needed some sincere advice on what I needed to do next, and it was only one person I held that much trust in.

～

District 12
College Park

PULLING my car in front of the two-story home, I killed the engine and took a few seconds to think in silence. My entire world seemed to crash down in a matter of seven hours after it took me over a decade to build my whole platform and foundation. I was lost, something I never gave a person the satisfaction of hearing from my mouth, but it was more than true. I was at my weakest, and the only option I had at this stage was releasing the true demon in me.

Climbing out of my car, I proceeded up the porch, ringing the doorbell once. It wasn't even ten seconds that passed before Taki answered the door with her baby .380 Auto in hand.

"Rude, what the fuck... come in." She grabbed me by the arm, pulling me inside.

After securing all the locks back on her door, she faced me before giving me a genuine hug. I could smell the scent of her vanilla coconut lotion coming from her skin, and the warmness of her flesh soothed me at the moment.

"Rude, I'm so sorry. I heard about Shanti. I'm just lost for words right now," she said sincerely, leading me to the couch to take a seat.

Taki was my best friend. She had always been since the seventh grade. Not only did she not hesitate to tell me when I was fucking up, she stood firm by my side even through all my bad decisions. Her red skin was covered with tattoos, and her curly, black hair and hazel eyes would put you in the mind of the singer Khelani. She was a positive girl, not to mention a math whiz. Her skills for calculating and investing paper was the main reason she became one of my close associates. Her temper could go left field sometimes, but she was one that I could trust with my life.

"I don't know what to do, Taki. This shit just doesn't seem real. Everyone knows places of business are off limits, and with my lady being across the district working, she should've been off limits too. They slaughtered her like this shit had been green lighted from Lo himself."

"Rude Boy, you know that Lo wouldn't violate those rules. He's the one that put them in place. He's not gonna break that code, not even for himself. Not to mention the punishment he enforces on the ones who can't give an explanation if the rules are broken. I should know cause I've worked around him for the past two years. Someone is gonna have to answer about Shanti being touched. So, don't blow your cool until you get word on what he's gonna do."

"That's the fucking problem, Taki. Sitting around waiting for an answer is gonna stir up some bigger shit on my plate. Her father has been calling me for the past two hours, and he's all the way in fucking Nigeria. I can't even fix my mouth to tell this man she's gone. Even worse, that I don't have the motherfucker responsible for it. He's gonna want a soul."

Pulling the Garcia Vega from my Gucci hoodie pocket, I sparked it, inhaling deeply on the Blue Cheese Kush. Weed was one of my biggest stress relievers, but I had been knocking down blunt after blunt within the last three hours, and the high still couldn't override the pain.

Taki grabbed my chin, forcing me to look at her. "You will get through this, and everybody that was involved will get spanked in the end for going against the grain, but if you let yourself fall now, all your hard work will be in vain, and you won't get to avenge her name. You have one of the most dangerous crews in Atlanta. They will get to the bottom of this. Just don't lose faith."

Nodding in silence, I leaned over, planting a quick kiss on her cheek.

"Thank you, Taki. Can you please do me one favor?"

She looked as if she was in deep thought for a minute. "Yes."

"I want a sit down with Lo within the next few weeks."

"Rude, you know that I can't just ask for a sit down out of the blue. Lo has to request it."

"Taki, please? I wouldn't ask if I felt that you couldn't handle it. At least try for me. I love you." I stood to my feet, placing my hoodie over my head.

She gazed into my eyes, wanting to say more, but I could tell that her mind and her body were in different places, and that was my cue that it was time to peel.

"Okay, Rude Boy."

"One more thing."

"What?"

"Cut off all the lights in the house and I'll be back through tomorrow."

"Why do you always want all the lights off before you leave, boy? You be moving like you Blade The Day Walker or some shit." She stared into my emotionless face before walking over to the power breaker in her hallway.

I blew her a light kiss before she hit the circuit, causing the house to go pitch black. I removed my Glock from my waist and exited out the back door of her crib in a flash. Before I could make it all the way back to my car and crank the engine, her lights were back on, and I was pulling back off into the streets of Atlanta.

CHAPTER TWO

Polar
Seven Hours Ago

After trying to call my arrogant ass boss for the fifth time, I knew that I was in the best position to make my own move and have this bitch ass nigga, Rude Boy, begging to me on his knees. I never liked moving on my own accord, but after I received the voicemail for the last time, I gave my loyal killer, Joker, the okay to proceed with our plan. After finding out that Rude's girl was working at Lucky's tonight, I had one of my personnel let us through the back door. Besides, I ran District 10, and it wasn't much of nothing I couldn't make happen. When Joker and I made it to the dressing room, this bitch came strolling out, and her appearance couldn't be mistaken. I stepped in front of her before she could move past me.

"You Shanti. Rio, right? Rude Boy's girl."

"Uh, damn, nigga, you just nearly bumped into me, fucking up my pretty bitch mode, and no, Shanti is in the dressing room getting ready to go on stage, and please don't keep saying that bitch is my twin. She looks like me, not the other way around."

I wanted to reply back, but once I looked hard enough, I could see the difference. It was awkward because Rio's name was being called to the stage just as we were standing around mentioning her name.

"Well, I guess you wouldn't mind catching the stage for her for a few minutes while I go in and holla at her?"

"What? My damn pleasure. I might make me a cool two Gs before you done talking," she replied, heading to the front of the club toward the stage.

I nodded to Joker before I entered the dressing room.

"If anybody tries to come in, kill 'em," I ordered before making my way inside.

My eyes landed on her standing in front of a chair that rested in front of a long mirror. Once I looked her up and down, I knew the stripper bitch I just interrogated wasn't lying.

"Excuse me, you don't suppose to be back here. Any special dance requests from me are done in the VIP section. I don't care how much money you got."

I smiled, showing my perfect thirty-two. My open face golds shined to perfection. Opening the top button to my all-white Louis Vuitton peacoat, I allowed the handle of my Ruger Xd9 to show, and her entire posture switched.

"Please think before you pull a country ass move and get shot in the head, baby girl. First, I wanna speak my peace, and after that, we gonna take a little ride to handle some affairs. Me and your man, Rude Boy, having some issues, and I figured that you could assist."

She lowered her pretty ass hazel eyes at me like a devil but listened very well to my instructions. "What do you want from me? And if you have anything stupid on your mind dealing with me, I suggest you cut your own head off cause Rude will kill you just for making this attempt," she threatened.

Before I could even ponder on what I needed to say, a sound of light gunshots could be heard coming from the front of the club, catching me off guard. I saw the bitch, Rio, flinch as if she was going to make a run for it, and my backhand collided with her jaw, knocking her unconscious. I wasted no time snatching her up into my arms, heading for the door.

Joker looked back at me when I stepped out of the dressing room.

"I don't know what the fuck is the dillio in the front, but it can't be good," he mentioned with his gun in hand.

"I see that. I heard shots. Just lead me through the back exit so we can get this bitch out of here."

We quickly made our way through the back exit door again. I couldn't help but stare down at this little bitch, Rio, feeling all light in my arms. She really was a bad motherfucker. I just hoped the boss didn't have any plans of killing the bitch because after Rude was gone, I was going to take lil one for myself.

$$\sim$$

Rude Boy
Dunwoody, Ga.

IT WAS EARLY the next morning when I cracked open my eyes to see the sunrays shining through my windows. I felt like my fucking brain was beating through the side of my head from the migraine and not sleeping. All I could think about was Shanti.

We had been living in our new home for the past two months, and our life had just become beautiful when my woman accepted me to be her husband for the rest of her life. We weren't pressed for money because we had plenty. We were strong with our position and the reputation alone. My weight was saluted in the city of Atlanta. Jumping up, I caught my baggy eyes in the reflection of the marble oak body mirror staring at me. I looked depressed and angry, but that was the energy I chose to hide. It was hard to admit, and the demon within me was breaking out the cage with every minute that ticked pass.

Tossing on a clean Calvin Klein shirt, I slid on my slippers and headed downstairs. My elegant home was laced on both floors. Marble French tile, six bedrooms, five baths, and the most luxurious features of lavishness that money could buy. Seventy-inch plasmas were mounted in each room. The best art paintings, antique statues, and the fastest engines that could be placed inside a foreign occupied a space inside our four-car garage.

Niggas knew me by Rude Boy. I was from Kingston, Jamaica, born and raised, six foot even, with a nasty habit for murder. When I first arrived from the island, I made it known that I would chop up any man that stepped into my lane, and I still held that promise fifteen years later. My money basically came from my business of exotic marijuana and some of the most potent ecstasy that touched the city. Money wasn't an issue, and I used it wisely to get ahold of whatever I needed and whomever I wanted.

Stepping down into my living room area, I sat down on the French-made leather sofa. My young killer, JoJo, also my best assassin, came down the stairs, entering the room directly behind me. JoJo was a necessity in my business because he was able to make large problems disappear in very small ways. It was never loud but always messy enough to leave a message. He was practically an expert when it came to using any gun but was even more deadly with a knife.

JoJo was quiet. I met him at the age of sixteen when he had nothing. He was homeless, searching for a way to survive. I never knew that he would get more bodies under his belt than myself, but I took him in and gave him his first mission not even three weeks later. He took care of his contract with ease, but I also noticed that he had a habit of snorting meth.

Time after time, he would smoke a cigarette, but his biggest problem was that sack. It was hard for me to tell him not to do it. Eventually, it was one of the only payments he would accept to do a kill for me. The other was money to take care of his basic needs, as in clothes and specific foods. I never knew too much about his background, but once I saw his dedicated loyalty to me for business, I moved him in and made sure he never wanted for anything.

He sat on the couch across from me with a Tommy Hilfiger hoodie over his head. A Ruger P89 was dangling from the pocket, and a cigarette was between his lips. He only nodded with a look that asked me mentally if I was okay. Shaking my head, I folded my arms.

"I need answers, JoJo. I want fucking answers."

"Whatever you tell me to do, Rude, it'll be written."

I listened to his response, knowing I didn't have to speak anymore. JoJo was my apprentice. He was undeniably the one who'd gotten me through all the nastiest and grimiest moments since I made him a part of my team. So, my honor of making sure he was good in every way was my promise.

My doorbell ringing broke my trance. I immediately moved to get up, but JoJo took the initiative and headed for the front entrance of my home, gun in hand. As I waited to see who the fuck was showing up to my pad so early in the morning, my heart skipped a beat when I noticed the two-armed Nigerian soldiers' step through in unison. My mind was telling me this moment would come, but I never knew the second when he would actually arrive.

JoJo stepped back into the living room, along with six other guards and Shanti's father, Hakim Malik Yustafa, the general of the Nigerian army. I immediately stood to my feet, bowing to acknowledge the royal highness.

"Sir, pardon me for being so unprepared."

He waved his hand to his men to move aside and made his way straight toward me. His eyes matched mine.

"Khalifa, you have failed and obviously look to be weak, and don't undermine when I say weak, son, because I mean it in every form I speak. I've come way from the country of my home. The same country me and your father fought side by side to save and earn an easy way of leadership for our generations to hear that my only daughter is dead. Now, you look me in the eyes and give me one, only one," he held up a finger to my face sternly, "one damn reason why I allowed you to accept the bondage of my daughter if you couldn't do something as simple as protecting her?"

"Father, I swear…"

"Don't swear! Don't you dare… Khalifa! Shanti is dead. So, before you speak something that isn't true, value your life as you still stand here, boy! Cause, right now, I don't know how to see you as my family. That is what I can swear, or Allah can rip my heart out and feed it to the sharks!" His voice boomed throughout my living room.

"I understand, Father. I promise that I am working every second, with every breath in me. I swear on my soul may you be rid of me if I do not bring the perpetrator's head to you mounted on a trophy in gold." I spoke, feeling the tears drop from my eyelids.

His hand shook uncontrollably, and his chest heaved with the anger of a lion. He wouldn't blink nor would my killer, JoJo, stop clutching on his pistol with every second he watched the tension grow. Mr. Yustafa accepted me like a son at the age of ten when I first met Shanti in Jamaica living with her mother, a woman who I cherished and had no heart to face at the present time. He saw the devotion and strength that I shared for his daughter, and because of my father, he allowed me to stand as her king, only if I vowed to protect her to my last dying day. I had failed miserably.

"Khalifa, I can't go home to her mother with no answers, so if you say you're my son, I want blood… enough blood to fill the Nile river. You tear down this city and paint her name in these streets or consider yourself erased from this bloodline. I will accept nothing less," he ordered before tapping the side of my head with his index finger.

As Mr. Yustafa and his soldiers left my home, I sat back on the couch, pondering on my next move. My next step was to put Polar's bitch ass in the ground. I needed to bring the Kiss Squad to an end, and I wasn't about to stop until their blood was flowing through my hands.

JoJo came to my side, touching my shoulder, causing me to look up at him.

"What do you want me to do, Rude?"

"I want you to make them pay. Make them regret ever fucking with the wolves of this city."

As usual, he didn't respond but nodded and headed back up the stairs. It was mutual feelings when it came down to wanting the ups in Atlanta, but my main objective now was pure revenge. I wanted them to feel how I felt, and I was going to make sure they understood that if one of mine got touched, we were willing to risk ourselves in order to get even. Whatever it took.

CHAPTER THREE

Polar
District 10, Zone 3
Washington Road

As I sat on the hood of my car, puffing on the loaded Backwood blunt, two of my top shooters, Tizo and Nino, pulled up directly beside me. I was counting a stack of paper and trying to put a play together on how I was about to get my next dollar. My biggest problem at the moment was this bitch, Shanti. I had yet to tell the boss that she was just sitting in the basement of my house alive because the news of her being dead had spread so far that I didn't need anything to erupt back in my face. So, I decided to keep everything at bay to see how things would play out in my favor.

Sure, the boss would be mad, feeling that a major step was knocked out of Rude Boy's foundation. It was even better knowing that I had the advantage he was unaware of. The life of this trick he craved so much. If it was up to me, I was going to shove my dick in her and make the bitch my baby mama for the hell of it. Until then, I had the ball in my court.

"Have y'all heard anything today?" I asked, looking up at them both.

Nino smiled. "You would've been the first person to know, my nigga. Ain't no reason for worrying about that now, boss man. We've set the standards, and all that red light, green light shit is over with. Them bitches deserve to get the nasty end of the business. Kiss Squad supposed to be on top. Erasing these bitches one by one. It's our world for real."

I cracked a smile, knowing that he had a point in a way, but in the end, my deal was received. I was going to iron the district with no mercy, here and in the afterlife. I continued to get more recognition and authority for power. I was never prepared to be touched, but it was a dog-eat-dog type of city, so I only had to bite as hard as I barked, and the rest would be handled.

"I'm asking because it's never enough room for security. As long as we stay ahead, we don't have to worry about anybody slipping through the cracks on us. I'm a man of persistence, and it hasn't failed me as long as I been working."

It was crazy because right after the words left my mouth, a familiar two-door Mercedes Benz coupe pulled up on the side of the curb across the street from us. We all focused our attention in that direction because it was only a few associates that could cross down my street, but the sun was still out, so it was no telling who we had visiting the hood.

When Bonnie's fine ass stepped out from behind the wheel, my radar immediately went off. Not only was she Rude Boy's most loyal female within his squad, but she was one that understood business. One that could deliver a message for me exactly how it needed to be said and done. Her ass was on fleek, clothes hugging all her curves. She was dressed in a Moschino shirt and a pair of matching black jeans.

On her feet, she sported a pair of pink Moschino slides. She was really one of the best-looking bitches out here running around the trenches. Her blonde afro was picked out neatly, like she was the leader of a pro-Black movement. She wasn't a slut for sure, but once again, she was on this nigga, Rude Boy's squad. I snapped my fingers, and my goons immediately went into motion.

They moved swiftly across the street before she could make her way into the nigga, Beans' building. He was a civilian, one that had a fool connection on the cocaine and guns, but Rude Boy was his main man. He still dealt with the oppositions on the back end to show that it wasn't any beef or favoritism, and, for that respect, Lo stamped it that he wasn't to be touched.

Just as Tizo and Nino reached Bonnie, I watched her reach inside the zipper of her purse.

"Hold up, lil mama, don't pull. We come in peace." I assured her with my hands high.

Tizo and Nino had already pulled their guns, but I could see it on Bonnie's face that she was ready to go out with a bang if we decided to seal her fate at that moment.

"It ain't no such thing as peace between us, Polar, and it never will be, especially after what you just did to my girl, Shanti."

"I have no idea what you're talking about, and I truly don't give a fuck, sweetie. I'm only sliding up on you to give you a proposition, one that I think you might want to consider."

She mugged me evilly, trying her best to keep her gangsta composure. I couldn't even act like I wasn't digging that shit because it was nothing like a stand-up ass woman, especially a bad one at that. Her only problem was the side she had chosen, and that meant shit was fair game when it came to folding anyone that wasn't on the winning side.

"Listen, Polar, I don't want any problems. I'm here to pick up my shipment, and I'm gonna be on about my way. This is your district, and nobody is trying to compete with you for it. It's just business, and unless business gets violated, we shouldn't have nothing to speak about," she spat back before heading up to Beans' crib.

I sat back, thinking about how I was about to make this bitch, Rude Boy, bow down to my fucking feet. I had to acknowledge the real when

I saw it. The Jamaican boy was a top-notch shooter, and his crew was just as deadly as mine. We both held major portions of the city in our grasp, and it benefited to the best for both sides. He was relentless when it came to being a boss, and it was one of the main reasons I knew how to step when it came to us bumping heads.

Unfortunately, the city wasn't big enough for the both of us. I wanted all the power the Kiss Squad had to offer. We were the definition of murder. Killing was so simple. It was a motto that I stood on since I built my team, and the fun I was issuing out was just the beginning. I wanted the entire Chaos City, and I wasn't going to stop until it was mine.

$\sim$

JoJo
District 10
10:15 p.m.

PEEKING my head from behind the rundown townhome, I watched Polar drive off in his white Cadillac Escalade truck. Two of his rookie soldiers stood off in the middle of the street as if they owned the world. My mission was simple, avenge Shanti's death by any means, but I was ordered to do it quietly and messily. District 10 was operated by Polar, mainly the Kiss Squad and the most ruthless gang affiliates in Atlanta. I didn't care about any one of them. I didn't fear anything, especially any place, thing, or being that went against what Rude Boy stood for. I owed him my life, and I would always be the havoc that rose out of the word *chaos*.

Sliding my hoodie over my head, I slowly made my way across the street. The two guards never recognized me until I was far beyond their boundary lines. I tapped the first one on his shoulder, and by the time he turned around to face me, my fist collided with his throat, crushing his windpipe. As he fell to the ground, the next casualty reached for his gun but was too slow. I raised my Glock 23 pistol, squeezing the trigger twice, hitting him once in the head and another in the heart.

Boom! Boom!

He was dead before his body could touch the ground. Slowly walking up to the stash house, I calmly entered and scanned the residence immediately. Three armed men stood around nervously, and all of them seemed to be frozen in action at my unexpected appearance.

I raised my gun, shooting the closest to me in the throat. I caught the next with a shot to the leg and two slugs to his face.

Boom! Boom! Boom!

The last worker stood in front of me, trembling for dear life. I walked up to him and casually removed the gun from his hand. I was calm when I spoke. "I need you to bag up all the money and merchandise, so I can be on my way. If you even hide twenty-five cents from going into that bag, I will replace that value with your head. Now!" I yelled with wide eyes.

He stumbled and stuttered, moving around like a fucking rabbit. He stuffed tons of bills and drugs inside, and within two minutes, he was back in front of me, holding it out for me to take. I smirked before sending a bullet through his right eye, watching him crumble against the wall that stood behind him.

Boom!

Everything in the space grew quiet, and I stood still, listening for any form of movement around me. Death was the loudest in the air, and one of my missions was complete. Pulling out my phone, I snapped a picture of all my victims one by one and left back out of the front door. An all-black 2024 Expedition truck pulled up in front of the house as I came down the driveway. The money was strapped on my back, and I concealed my pistol on the side of me in case I had to take care of a dispute before I could leave the scene.

A dark skinned, young hustler stuck his head out from the back window, eyeing me curiously. "Say, my man, I'm looking for Polar. Is he in?"

"Yeah, he is. Just go on up to the door. Someone will answer," I lied while walking back across the street, not waiting for him to reply. I jumped the fence that sat behind the townhome and came out on the next intersecting road. Climbing into the all-grey Lexus sedan, I pulled slowly into traffic and headed back for Rude's spot. I needed to make them see his pain. I planned to shed as much blood as needed in order to get that point across. This was what I lived for.

CHAPTER FOUR

Rude Boy

I had wrapped up a phone call with a few of my associates from the Virgin Islands whose help I needed. Even though I had the manpower to war with anyone I chose, I intended to plan thoroughly in case things started to go sour. Bonnie entered the room, forcing me to look up at her disgruntled face. She rarely looked frustrated, so I knew something had to be wrong.

She tossed my shipment on the floor with a hand on her hip. "We need to talk, Rude, now!" she said with stern aggravation.

"What's going on? What happened, Bonnie?" I asked before Daffy, and I gave her our full attention.

"The problem is Polar. I went to pick up the order, and he and a few of his shooters pulled up on me. I was alone, and he was trying to press me on some shady shit. I don't even feel comfortable going back to pick up the shipment from here on out. He could've had me killed, Rude," she stressed with a hint of worry in her tone.

"Why didn't you just call one of us?" Daffy stepped in.

"Right, pull my cell from my pocket and get a bullet to the head. Maybe I could have tried to warn you of my death afterwards. Don't act like it's not a fucking procedure, Daffy. I can only do so fucking much."

"Fine, from now on, I'll handle all the pickups during sunrise out in District 10. Polar isn't fucking God, and he damn sure ain't gon press on this crew."

"No," I butted in quickly. "From now on, I'm gonna go handle the plays with Beans in 10. For right now, we just have to make our alliances strong as possible because eventually, Lo will have to grant me Chaos City day, and soon as I get the chance, I'm gonna make everyone that mounted up against us see that they shouldn't have," I stated before dialing a number on my cell.

After a few rings, Taki's voice fell smoothly through the line.

"Rude?"

"I need you to try and make that happen for me in the next few days, or we might have to take matters into our own hands."

"I told you, Rude Boy, you have to keep patience with this, or it could turn out bad on your end. Even if you're right. You're thinking off emotions right now, and you don't need that."

"This city is run by Lo, but he doesn't run me or my crew; neither will he place boundaries on us when the law has clearly been broken. We will kill twenty-four hours of the day until he grants my pass for Shanti's blood. My family is involved now, Taki. It's deeper than just me," I pleaded for her understanding.

"I can't promise anything, Rude, but I'll do anything to try and make it happen. Just don't do anything crazy." She ended the call.

The knock at my hotel room door threw off my train of thought. Daffy opened it up to Cinco moving inside in a hurry.

"We got a problem downstairs." He alerted me with a blunt face.

"What kind of problem?" I asked.

"Cops, they wanna talk to you. They're down at the front desk holding them off, but I don't know for how much longer, man."

"Everybody, load up. I need all shipments to the main house and all the cash dropped off to JoJo at the getaway. So, recruit some more skills cause I feel this war scratching at my flesh. Make sure y'all exit this property unnoticed. I got the cops," I ordered.

"I got ya, boss man. You know that." Cinco nodded before leaving to take the emergency exit stairs to the first floor.

I exhaled humbly, pressing the button for the elevator. After getting inside, I reached the bottom floor in sixty seconds. As soon as my eyes got a visual of the main entry, I spotted the two cop heads coming my way. They looked like a pair of dirty Feds from *Street Kings*, but I was always taught how to master my energy around the law. After all, they worked for the biggest animal in the city, so they didn't mind crossing you over. Before I could get a few feet from the elevator, they approached me quickly but not aggressively.

"Is there anything I can help you gentlemen with? I haven't done shit, so I'm not into the harassing, and I damn sure ain't got no warrants," I spat before either one could open their mouths.

"I'm Investigator Harris, okay? First off, we don't need a fucking warrant for shit when you're wanted for questioning about a murder. We need you to take a ride with us."

"Murder? Get the fuck outta here. I don't need to kill anybody for any reason when I have thousands of reasons that I'm allowed to kill a man for. That's bullshit!"

"We never said it was a man, asshole. I see why your name is Rude Boy; you're very disrespectful. Now, put your hands behind your back."

I obliged, holding in my rage. "I wanna speak to my lawyer, or my people will come speak differently." I threatened them both indirectly.

"Well, guess what, motherfucker? Lo doesn't give a fuck who you or your people are, so you take that up with the bullet that we're about to place in your head," he whispered low enough for only me to hear.

I jerked and fought with them for a second, but the cuffs and two men were too much. They fumbled with me but still pushed me out to their car in front of the hotel. Throwing me into the backseat, they climbed in the car and jumped into traffic. I sat back in the cruiser, knowing that this was beyond a set up.

"You idiots know that you're gonna die, right? I know you're not cops, so I'll let you live another year of your lives," I stated coldly with an evil grin.

The accomplice in the passenger seat pointed a gun at me through the cage bars.

"Listen here, dipshit, you'll die now if you keep popping all that shit. It's just a job, not personal. So, sit back and shut the fuck up!"

I kept calm and tried my best to pay attention to where I was heading. I had too much on my plate, and the target on my head was constantly out to spot me on any given day. Dying wasn't on my fucking agenda, so being evil was the only resolution when that energy came anywhere near my zone. The sound of a loud motor engine could be heard speeding up behind us just as the driver made a right on a one-way street. The impact of it smashing into the bumper caused us all to jerk.

"Who the fuck is that? I thought we had no tails." Fake officer number two panicked, looking back and forth in the side mirror.

"I don't know. Just speed the fuck up, Benny. Lose him."

I held on to the seats as tight as possible, closing my eyes with a small grin.

The car sped up until it was on the side of the police cruiser. Sliding over into the same lane, it smashed us harder, causing the vehicle to flip out of control. After sliding a great distance, I winced and clenched my jaw from the pain shooting through my side. The looks of the two phony officers were delusional, and seconds later, the chasing car pulled up directly beside us. I spotted the shoes stepping out from the driver's seat. The two gophers in the car with me slowly stirred around, trying to break free. The driver's door flew open, and JoJo placed two slugs into the driver's head.

Boom! Boom!

His head opened up horribly before he snatched him out the seat, throwing him to the ground. The second fuck-up tried to make a break, but JoJo silenced him with one to the back of his head.

Boom!

"Rude, are you okay?" JoJo looked down at me. "What do you want me to do?"

"Ahh, shit!" I yelled, feeling pain shoot from my arm then throughout my entire body. I knew my arm had to be dislocated.

"Just take me to Taki's house and stay posted for me."

He tossed my arm around his shoulder and helped me to the passenger seat of his car. Jumping behind the wheel, he smashed off. We got as far away from the scene as possible and didn't want to be around the aftermath that took place. JoJo was unmerciful, which was why I never kept him too far away. I paved the way in my city, but my respect had me receiving the same back in return. Trust was dead with everybody. Blood was what I wanted, and I was about to take it.

As JoJo jumped on the expressway, gliding through the lanes, I was placing everything together in my head. It was all for Shanti. I was preparing my mind that I was about to die for it as well.

CHAPTER FIVE

Taki

After Rude Boy showed up to my house a few hours ago all busted up, I blasted him with a little too much emotion. Bandaging him up and making sure he was good on my end was the only relief to bring my energy back down to mellow. He was one of the only true friends I had. True enough, I'd always harvested deep emotions that I had never brought to his attention, but I'd always looked at myself as a valuable piece when it came down to him, and I wanted it to remain that way. The streets of Atlanta were a burning place for legends, a battlefield to destroy every ounce of competition that stepped in your area. It was a cycle of lose-lose, and no matter who felt they were stronger, everyone was going to reach the same place in the end when the smoke cleared.

"I just don't understand, Rude. All you have to do is let me see what I can do. You're gonna end up getting killed before anybody gets to find out the truth about anything."

"It's past that, Taki. Don't you understand? They killed Shanti, they coming for my head, and running ain't something that's in my blood. Do ya understand? I've built this shit brick by brick. I've made millions of dollars in this city, and I've also given millions of dollars to show that when one win, everyone can win. That's not the fucking love I'm receiving back. That blood clot, Lo, wants murder, and that's exactly what he's finna get!" he yelled, standing up from the chair he was resting in.

"Rude, if you go against Lo, everyone in this city will come for you. We won't be able to protect anyone. So, are all the lives of your loyal friends worth you thinking irrational at the moment? Huh? No, they aren't. I need you to calm down and listen to me. If not, you're gonna lose more than just Shanti," I stressed, folding my arms.

His killer, JoJo, just sat back against the wall, staring at me as I talked. His energy was always awkward to me. He never spoke, neither did he respect me as Rude Boy's associate. I just knew in my mind that, one day, we'd clash if our vibes continued to be indifferent toward each other.

Rude Boy stood at the end of my kitchen, staring out the patio window. He was destroyed, not just mentally but physically. He was capable of crashing on anything at any time, and I was afraid of that happening.

"You know, when me and Shanti were at home on days like this, we would always just sit back and think about what we wanted to do after this life. It's like we had so much planned, so much joy to find that we never got a chance to see. These motherfuckers have ripped my chest open and burned my heart, Taki. I am nothing without family. I'm nothing without my honor, and I am nothing without Shanti," he vented with hurt laced in his tone.

"Yes the fuck you are. You are everything and more when it comes to who you are. You think these bitches don't respect you... no, they fear and respect you, and that's something only you can take away from yourself, nobody else. You have to move smarter and better. You're the leader of the Wolf Gang. That position has held weight in this city since you arrived, and it's only gonna stay that way if you want it to." I got up and rubbed his shoulder.

"I'm lost on what to do."

"Well, think harder and in the meantime, I'm gonna request that Lo has a sit down with you, even if it takes a month. The best revenge is smooth and comes with patience. You will win in the end."

I watched him pull out his phone, and his fingers moved across the screen. Tucking the phone away, he placed his gun back on his hip and slowly slid his shirt back on then his jacket.

"Listen, Taki, this sit down is the only understanding I have left. It's the only thing that will show me Lo isn't behind this shit. If I can't get it after my woman has been killed, then that will tell me all I need to know. My problem will be with him, and I really don't care too much about how it turns out."

"But, Rude."

"No buts, Taki... tell him exactly like this. If I don't get the sit down and I mean soon, I'll come for him. Whatever it takes, whatever it cost. I will kill him." He assured before nodding at JoJo.

I watched them both leave my home and climb back into their car before leaving my street. I stood in the same spot, and rage took over me. Raising my foot, I stomped the large glass table in the center of my living room to pieces, cutting my leg in the process. As I winced in pain, I sat back on the couch watching the thick blood trickle down my leg. A small smile danced on my face from the rush. My mind always tried to take control when this feeling came over me. I cared for Rude Boy, but he was more valuable to me than he knew. I refused to let him make the decision to lose, even if he made me stand in the way myself.

CHAPTER SIX

Rude Boy
Club Ellery's

Pulling up to the plaza on Campbellton Road, I pulled my car inside the entrance and stepped out with JoJo at my side. I was sore and aggravated, and after the talk with Taki earlier, a thought crossed my mind that I had to act on immediately. This city was big enough for everyone to eat, but just like any dog that got greedy, it would eventually turn on anyone to take it all. I was a dog that was ready to die before you stripped me down to nothing, and I was going to prove it. A known Cuban boss by the name of Kamo was a powerful source for any inside information, so I decided to pay him a visit.

He ran heroin, weapons, and trafficked women through his restaurant and other businesses. He was a dangerous man, and his workers were menaces, Cuban killers that meant every word that came out of their mouths. Even after all the ties between me and Sami, I never had a chance to meet him personally. It was always through a middleman, so my reach only stretched so far when it came to receiving any help directly from him. Today was the day that would change.

Waking inside the luxury nightclub, the music played softly through the speakers. The lights were dim, and a few people moved around serving guests and entertaining at the bar. I spotted Kamo's assistant, Sami, talking to a bartender. I moved toward him and was immediately stopped by a roughneck Cuban who was puffing on a cigar. He gripped a black handgun at his side while looking me and JoJo up and down. JoJo pulled his pistol, matching his energy. Before any words or bullets were exchanged, I stepped in between the two.

"I know we showed up without notice, but this is still my district. We just came to speak with Sami, and then we'll be on our way," I said as if debating wasn't an option.

He mugged harder, and before his words could leave his mouth, Sami turned around from the bar with a smile.

"Rude Boy, if it isn't my favorite negotiator in the state. What a surprise. Is there anything I can do for you?" He walked over to me and shook my hand firmly.

"We need to talk."

He raised an eyebrow, looked back at a few of his guards, and nodded in compliance before leading me to a table. JoJo stood up behind me with his eyes scanning the entire room. The same angry Cuban we encountered first was right beside Sami with a look of death staining his face.

"It's been a while since I've even spoken to you, Rude. I know that you never appear out of thin air without reason, so this shall be interesting, or will it?" he mocked as his waiter came and poured us both a glass of champagne.

I thought about what I wanted to say before I spoke. The wrong thing could make shit tense, and I didn't need that. "Listen, Sami, things in the city have been a little shaky for me lately, and I don't mean to make the random approach, but I don't trust many, and my options are running low. A few days back, my wife, Shanti, was murdered out in District 10."

"Polar?" He shook his head with grief.

"Yes, and right now, there is no room for understanding. Lo is allowing Atlanta to crash with the lawless behavior of these district leaders, and it has broken a chain that has been bound for a long time. I still haven't received a sit down for the death of my loved one, and friction is stirring up by the minute as the days go on with no conclusion. I'm grateful to you and Kamo for the way we've conducted business thus far, but now, I need you guys' assistance more than anything."

"And what assistance do you speak of, Rude? Trust and believe that we are appreciative of all your loyalty, but when it comes down to a standpoint on business or these organizations, nothing — and I mean nothing — will interfere with what the Cubans have going on. Not now, not never. So, what is this favor that you're asking?" He twirled his hands around slowly, trying to make out what exactly it was that I needed.

"I want you guys to stand beside me if Chaos City is granted from Lo. The Cubans and Wolf Gang have never had any bad run-ins and this decision , as I said, would be respected if it can be granted… I also need to meet Kamo. Personally," I said with a straight face.

Sami burst out in a fit of laughter, slapping his hand on the table as if there was something comical about my statement. I watched his bodyguard clutch his gun tighter, and before he could move, JoJo closed the space in between them, shooting a hard right jab to his gut. Grabbing him by the hair, he placed the pistol to the top of his skull, waiting for my word. Sami's face balled up quickly, slightly frightened from the sudden movement of my killer. The rest of his workers pulled their guns but were calmed by his hand, waving them to stand down.

"Argh, motherfucker!" The Cuban on the ground grunted in pain but respected the energy of JoJo's gun.

"You make a request from us then disrespect me in my restaurant as if we are enemies." Sami intertwined his fingers slowly. "Rude Boy, I can assure you that playing this game will only end nasty, and I mean nasty as you can possibly think," he threatened.

Exhaling calmly, I picked up the champagne , smelling it lightly before tossing it into his face. The splash of the liquid caught him off guard. His bodyguards tensed, and JoJo, snatched the Cuban's head back harder, forcing him to howl out in pain.

"Don't do it," JoJo mumbled in a low tone.

Once again, Semi calmed his shooters while wiping his face, and he glared at me with hatred filled eyes.

"So much has been lost since the times of different territories have been divided, Rude Boy, and I'll make this clear when I say it. If Shanti's death hasn't sparked any pandemonium for blood to be spilled. Then it will never happen . I've been knowing Lo for a long time, and Kamo is strict on how he deals when it comes to choosing sides. It's the reason we have lasted so long. He will likely deny your request, and it will still leave us at odds due to the emotion you've shown here today."

"Well, maybe you need to think about your life when you speak on his business because I know what's needed to get to small guys like you. As I said, I have love and respect for this family, but this is what I need. I can't allow this to happen, and I won't. You can set me up with Kamo myself, and I'll explain what I have to, or you can die but time is running out, and settling for the lesser option is not up for debate. Can you make it happen? If not, my mind will tell me how I'm leaving out of here and if this business of yours remains standing in a territory I built."

He clenched his jaws together, seething. His response was expected. I also expected him to know that this would end my way or whichever way God saw fit if he didn't have an answer for me within the next few minutes.

"I'll handle it. One of my men will reach you when it's time. If any boundary is crossed again with us like such," he pointed down to his worker who JoJo still had hemmed up, "we will all die for the sake of what we believe in. That's on my mother, Maria. May her soul be cooled as it burns in hell."

"I hope it chills until it cracks. I just want to keep the bond mutual. My request is one that can be respected or denied. It truly doesn't matter to me whichever is chosen." I glared at him with no emotion.

"Have a good day, Rude Boy. And be sure to never bring this

asshole right here back into my fucking place of business ever again." He pointed at JoJo to release his henchmen.

"Let 'em go, JoJo," I ordered before preparing to leave. "Thank you, Sami. I know that you may not see it, but I'm only doing what's best, or we will all lose."

"We all will lose one day regardless, Rude Boy. It's a part of what we do. It's like a birthright. May our days continue to last long," he said, standing back with his killers beside him.

"Indeed." I walked out of the club with JoJo beside me.

"Are you sure we won't have to worry about these guys, Rude?" JoJo asked as he ushered me all the way to my car door with his alert eyes scanning everyone and everything around us.

"I'm sure. We are the predators right now, and motherfuckers know that. We just have to be willing to show it."

My assassin jumped in the passenger seat, and I pulled swiftly out of the parking lot, heading down Delowe Drive for the expressway. Some of my close friends were still out here in this city, but with how shit was turning out, I didn't trust anything. I made enough money to go against anybody that opposed me, but the wolf in me always thought for more than just myself. Those humanly and hearted feelings of love were pouring out of me by the second, and rage was about to be my new face.

"What do you think we need to do? What if Lo doesn't agree to this, then what?" he asked me sincerely while watching our rearview.

To be honest, I didn't know how to answer his question, but I was ashamed to admit it because it just wasn't a trait of mine.

"I'm searching for snakes. Some just ain't right, and I can feel it down in my stomach. This just doesn't seem real, lil bro. I'm snatching up my bread from the businesses we got jumping. Once it's secured, I'll set up new plans for somewhere that's far from here. After I know everybody is safe, I'm shutting this city down street by street. We gonna slide through all the stash spots and clean house if shit ain't right. I haven't even been to my directing classes in like a month. About a year back, I started to work on my dreams ,and also leave the game behind. I had a few friends in the film directing area and started to attend a small school. Shanti's situation paused me. I just lost my entire vision, and I wanted it back with a little more," I replied before falling back into my own thoughts.

All I could see was Shanti's face when I thought about my current position. My soul had been snatched from me, and there was no other female that could match the purity and love my Queen had given me. Blood filled my mind, and each day I breathed, I was going to show the nightmare that victims prayed to never come.

CHAPTER SEVEN

Polar
District 8
Greenbriar Mall

After hanging up the phone on my disrespectful ass boss, I pulled into Greenbriar to conduct my weekly meet-up with the squad at the IHOP for brunch. We didn't step out much unless it was in the clubs or establishments where we held our business. I was up on the scoreboard and needed to keep all this shit in line to ensure my plan was executed effectively. Stepping out of my car, I watched my Kiss Squad steppers walk over to my truck.

"I'm glad all y'all could make it. Well, we all know it's no gain if you ain't feeling no pain, and lately, this shit has been hurting me to my fucking stomach. One of my spots was just hit hard. I could care less about the money, but the soldiers I just lost has made a bad situation with some people that I care for dearly."

I looked at Tizo, Joker, and my ruthless young killer, Nino, to make sure we were all on the same page. I needed to make it known that we were fresh out of mercy when it came to going against what we stood on. In my mind, I had a feeling that it could've been Rude Boy cranking up the retaliation for his bitch. It still wasn't known that I had this girl tied up in my basement. Things were getting a little too shaky to even expose something so fragile. Until I was sure no one was making a move against my boss' movement, things would remain quiet.

"I mean this when I say it, and I can't stress it enough. **Death is as easy as a kiss**. That's why we do what we do. If anybody look like they doing the wrong thing, we need to bury them hatchets and clear out a little of this smoke. I just don't wanna see this blow up in our faces in the long run."

"You know we can't just kill in other districts, Polar. Lo will send everything he has at us for breaking any code. Kiss Squad will be on everybody's radar. Do you really wanna do that?" Nino asked as if my word wasn't bond alone.

"Nigga, I'm the one who killed the first sixteen motherfuckers to stamp Kiss Squad in the streets the deep way. I'm sure whatever I say, even if I couldn't remember it, is solid. Killing is so simple, Nino. That's the way it is, and that's the way it'll always be," I spat, looking around at all my shooters. They were twelve of my best, but Joker, Tizo, and Nino were my weapons. I even had a few animals in the clutch that not too many knew about. It was all about perfect timing, and I had mastered it.

"What about Rude Boy?" Tizo asked directly behind my statement, like something I said was misunderstood.

"Fuck Rude Boy. If anything, they better not get caught trimming in our districts or anywhere around our personal residences. Fuck the Wolf Gang and all them fake ass thugs they running with. Soon, I'll be the king of this city, and I'll show everybody how to be elite. Look around us, my guy. We can't lose."

Tizo looked as if he soaked in what I said, as he walked off toward his car. in my mind, I didn't trust him as far as I could see him. He was already the boss' little pet from my view, and I never had too many good moments on getting him to listen without running back and telling everything to the same person that paid me. I was good for me with the hitters I had on one accord. Nothing could get around me, and I was also prepared to do whatever necessary to keep it that way.

"If that's how you feel, we need to swerve; then it's good. I just know how Lo is when it comes to bumping heads. It doesn't matter to me." Nino shrugged his shoulders, not caring about the outcome.

"Lo just make the rules; he ain't out there pushing that law in the streets himself for real. That nigga's a bitch for all I know. Let's get back to getting that money. Keep the drug houses moving, steal every fucking luxury car you can, and kiss any bitch to sleep that goes against what we standing on."

I watched all of them nod with understanding before we headed inside the IHOP to smash down on whatever we could before sliding back into the streets. I wanted to reign with the souls of the city in my hands, and I didn't mind taking a few losses just to beat the bosses.

∼

Taki
City Hall
10:14 p.m.

AFTER MAKING it down to District 1 in downtown Atlanta, I arrived at the city hall where Lo attended to most of his businesses and problems that he wanted taken care of. His hands were involved in every business, and he didn't hesitate to deal with people that were late on paying their taxes out of their districts. He was the devil — more than the devil when it came down to the so-called leaders of the chaotic city. It was a disaster as a masterpiece, and Lo held on to that painting firmly.

Walking into the office, Lo was already in a meeting with a few other business associates and connections that he worked with on different levels. His slim build was dressed in a gray men's Dior suit with matching dress shoes. His hair was combed to perfection, and he was the next best thing to a Black man in a white man's body. Lo was brutal and conniving when it came to winning. Truthfully, what rich, white guy wasn't? He held the throne on the battlefield and used all of his power to suck up everything that was in the path of what he wanted.

"Good evening, Taki. It's wonderful that you decided to join us today. I need the numbers for all the districts within the past three months. It seems as if someone has been coming up short on their end, and that can't go unhandled."

"Understood, and if it's okay with you, sir, I would like to relay a request to you. It comes from District 7," I advised while preparing to give him the numbers he requested.

He stared at me for a few seconds, making me slightly uncomfortable.

"Taki, we both know that sit-downs have to go through a precise procedure. I can't be bias, neither can I break the rules just because it's District 7… that's Rude Boy if I'm correct. I'm sure whatever he has on his mind can hold off for a few weeks. We have something very delicate to deal with tonight," Lo responded, staring at the table of his political advisors and leaders.

One representative held the status for the north side of Atlanta. There were also leaders for the west, south, and east side. Each leader was responsible for keeping control of the smaller territories in order to remain seated as the representative for that side. These particular bosses were worth millions, and they held most of the city's affairs together like glue. I knew that this night had to be important for everyone to be in attendance. I also knew it was more important to make sure Rude Boy received justice for Shanti, or no one would be able to rest.

"His wife's life was taken inside of District 10 for no plausible reason. Chaos City rules specify in section four that all women and children are off limits when in another district zone regardless of war, conflicts, or enemy beef that is being enforced by any leader or district. She was killed at her job, Lo, and Rude Boy wants a sit-down to see how this is going to be handled." I forced myself to speak again.

Lo cut his words short before responding, as if he was pondering on my statement. "Hold that thought for one second. In regard to my table, I specifically picked you all because I felt that it was in you all's blood and mental to run these districts with an iron fist. The duties that come with being a representative of this city is the same critical effort that you have to put in being a bum on the street surviving from death and starvation. You put your all into it until you can't put anything else."

"That's hard to do when we barely can keep peace around this hellhole. You expect us to run these sides of Atlanta with a bunch of fools off the leash to do whatever they please. It's never going to work, Angelo. You have become a madman with conducting this business under these conditions; we haven't." Ortiz, the representative of the north, spoke up behind him.

"Hard? We have been running this city for over thirty years with politics, prisons, and even senseless drug trafficking to benefit all that we can to win around this state and remain at the top. We receive more revenue than four of the biggest states in the south put together. So, you mean to tell me that you didn't think there would be any kind of problem that would transpire from this eventually? There will always be bloodshed, there will always be violations, and that's because no one wants to be controlled. It's still in their nature, so count these losses as blessings. Any objections?" Lo looked around the room at the representatives.

"My thought still stands where it stands. I can't work in conditions like this..."

Lo removed a silenced pistol from his suit blazer, releasing two slugs into his head.

Pwet! Pwet!

Everyone jumped at Lo's swiftness. Nobody expected a representative's head to be blown off in a meeting by the man they were in partnership with. I was even startled a bit, but I didn't flinch, nor did I take my eyes off this nutcase. I didn't plan on dying from asking a question for the sake of Rude Boy. My life was more valuable than the average, and I had backup plans in case shit ever seemed sour.

The last three representatives sat quiet with the expression of a startled deer being hunted by an outrageous leopard. The fear was clearly instilled inside these weak motherfuckers. I knew Lo would have the seat replaced by another representative before morning.

"Does anyone else feel that way!? Does anyone feel that way at all?" He looked around the room, his eyes saying that he would kill anyone who had any objections.

Everyone shook their heads, and he placed the gun back in his jacket. On cue, Lo's clean-up crew quickly entered the room and began to wrap ole buddy in a casket of plastic, and Lo's eyes shifted to me. Catching his stare, I didn't know if I needed to go into life-or-death mode. Killing me damn sure wasn't going to be easy, but going at his ass was about to be simple.

"You tell Rude Boy; District 7 doesn't run my city. I make the rules, I enforce the rules, and when everyone dies off and the asphalt crashes, when it begins to regrow, these rules will still stand. Meeting granted. Three weeks. That's an extra seven days just because they're District 7. This matter is to be settled at the sit-down and not a minute before. Hopefully, that's understood."

"Understood." I walked toward the door with my .380 still tucked in my jacket pocket.

"Uhh, Taki?" Lo called out.

I turned, watching him eye my backside lustfully. I knew the Valentino jeans I had on hugged my curves, and my curly hair was always enticing to the nose when I stepped in his office. I never doubted the power of a woman, but I knew a man was only so tough to a soft piece of skin. Pussy that is. Lo couldn't help but to toss his anger around on people, but I was one he couldn't think about crossing. I knew every secret and every loop that could flip his Chaos City into my city.

"Yes?"

"Be sure word goes out to all districts. If dues are not met accurately, all rights for the district goes out. I'm raising the stakes ten percent."

I hated the threats and vain speaking he was forcing at the moment, but I knew that he could also make good on what he said.

"Understood."

I walked out of his office on a mission, and the vision of what he was about to do crossed my mind like a vivid dream. Lo was going to crash out this city until everybody was dead. He wanted to crash it all out, and the game that Rude Boy was playing right now was exactly what he needed.

CHAPTER EIGHT

Daffy

Feeling her bounce her juicy ass against my piece, I bit down on my bottom lip and leaned in with my strokes. She was so wet and tight. Her skin glowed from the light sweat that we had worked up over the past thirty minutes. Spreading her bubble booty, her cookie talked to me lightly as I mashed the d in as deeply as I could.

"Uhh… sss… damn, Daffy!" she moaned, feeling my shit touch the bottom of her stomach.

Bonnie wasn't just a friend to me; she was a teacher, a motivator, and a lover. We had been seeing each other for the past year or so, but we always kept our business on the low. We didn't need Rude Boy or anyone else in the crew feeling funny about our encounters. So, instead of putting our business on front street, we kept it under the radar.

Sliding out of Bonnie's warm, sweet box, I guided her fine ass on top of me. It didn't take long before she found her rhythm and bounced on top of me with perfection.

"Damnnn, baee... you deeep. You going deep!" she screamed out and scratched at the headboard.

The sound of her ass clapping against my gut had me ready to explode in her at any moment. Her sweet nectar spilled down my dick as I thrusted in and out of her. It was warm, and the tingles on the inside of my stomach started to grow. I slapped her ass and gripped her hips to match her rhythm.

"Sssss... right there, nigga!"

"Make that shit cum for me!" I grunted as she threw her ass back harder. I felt myself reaching my peak before exploding inside her walls. She rocked back and forth a few more times on top of me before climbing off and posting up beside me. I looked at her with lust filled, hooded eyes; she had me fucked up.

"You never cease to amaze me. I can't believe we've made it this far. Hope things remain the same. Let's cheers to that." She picked up the champagne flute from the nightstand and downed the last of the wine.

"Cheers to that." I smiled devilishly, got dressed, and rested my head.

Making my way down the main hall of the building, I made sure not to match anyone's gaze on my way out. I couldn't explain how I felt overall with the madness that was at hand. I just knew that this was a force neither Rude Boy nor Lo was prepared for. The city was about to grow chaotic.

～

Beans

District 10

MY TRAP HAD BEEN DOING numbers in the past few months, and by the grace of God, I had yet to go through any bullshit to put a crook in my business. I had bags of weed, keys of cocaine, and even a few ounces of meth. It sold the most in my spot and the main avenue that I did business with for anyone around the city. Lately, shit had been so hot that I slowed down on my movements.

"Pass me the drink, Sunny?" I asked my young thug that was head of my security.

I made sure all my young fools had paper and also made sure they stood on business. The city was different from back in the 2000s. Rules had changed, and law was being enforced thoroughly instead of being given and brought to justice. You were innocent until proven guilty. I was a boss hog, and that ran in my bloodline all the way back to Italy. My brother on my father's side was full Italian, and he made sure my income was sufficient enough to stamp me a wave in the spot.

"Look, nigga, you done drunk about a bottle ya damn self. We don't need no emotional Beans that might shoot us up at any second," Sunny laughed as he handed me the lean mixed with a bottle of apple juice. I took a sip, and the loud crash I heard burst through the door forced me to spit it out recklessly.

Pewt!

The silenced pistol sounded off, hitting Sunny in the center of his head, killing him instantly.

I watched his body fall to the floor, and my second bodyguard reached for his gun. A hunting knife slammed into his throat before his hand could pull, and my body was still frozen from what the fuck was going on. The shit was so fast, and by the time shit slowed down in my mind, I noticed that it was Tizo standing over me like a fucking zombie mounting over a victim.

"Tizo, wha—what the fuck is this?!" I blurted out, knowing that homie never came to see anybody if they weren't dying.

"Seems like your time has run out, puta." He spoke calmly with a sinister expression on his face.

"Wait a minute. You know Lo has me bonded. You can't do this!" I shouted, trying to stand up for my own life.

"Lo doesn't run this district, my friend," he replied, aiming his gun up at my face.

I closed my eyes, and the silenced whistle was the last thing I heard.

~

Shanti

I DIDN'T KNOW where the fuck I was, nor did I know how long I had been in this stinky ass basement. I knew for a fact that I had been kidnapped. I could only imagine what the fuck my husband, Rude Boy, was thinking. He had to be ripping the city apart if he knew that I was missing. I was tied down to a bedrail that was cemented against the wall. I was thanking God these nasty ass people hadn't taken my pussy or stripped me down until a bitch froze to death on this icicle ass floor. I was hungry, confused, and damn sho scared, but you better believe that it was my life over the next. Out of everything my man taught me, I learned to handle my business if it was necessary. I was making it back to him, one way or the other.

The noise of the locks shifting broke my train of thought. Looking up at the deadbolt door come open, I laid eyes on the same nigga that stepped into my dressing room that night. He was the last face I remembered. I immediately went into panic mode, slamming my back against the wall with my fists balled just in case I had to knuckle up with this big muthafucka.

He held up his hands, as if he was coming in peace. The smirk on his face was sly, but he kept his distance before speaking.

"Wassup, lil one? I see you've been laid out for a minute, but I didn't mean to hit you hard at all. Truthfully, I wasn't supposed to have you here; you're actually supposed to be dead, but your little twin at work got in the way of that."

"I don't know what you're talking about. You might wanna let me go. If my man finds out, there's no telling how he might chop you up to fucking pieces when he finds out you have me here!" I shouted, ready to drop tears.

"I know you might be angry right now, but I can promise you'll eventually get used to this. See, I saved you from my boss that wanted you dead, and if I wouldn't have done what I've done, you would be dead. So, show some gratitude, bitch. And for your husband, I can't say that he is so blessed like you. Turns out, the boss wants both of you gone; it looks like I'm up one favor," he said with a humble tone.

Hearing that Rude Boy was gone sent a shockwave through my body. I felt as if I wanted to quit breathing, trying to hold my balance against the wall.

"I don't believe you… he can't be."

"Oh, yeah, you might wanna take a look at your position, Mama. You only still here cause I ain't told nobody you here. Keep that shit wrapped around your brain." He walked out of the room.

Just as I started to roam through a million thoughts, he rushed back through the door and made his way in front of me. I stared down the cold barrel of a .357 revolver, and the look on his face was angrier than before.

"I should just go ahead and kill yo ass, shouldn't I?" He pressed the gun to the bottom of my cheek harshly.

"You do whatever you feel needs to be done. I will never feel weak under a weak ass man. My nigga will come for me," I spat, truly not knowing what position my man was even in.

He smirked at me before nodding and slowly making his way back to the door.

"Looks like I'm ya man now then, bitch. Get used to it," he replied before leaving out the door.

I didn't know how to feel; I didn't know what to think. So many feelings were rushing through me that I just instantly started to cry. I hated this life, and time after time, I tried to get Rude Boy to see where my mind was on the subject of staying in the streets and also risking so much between our life in this troublesome city. I just prayed that he was somewhere wondering if I was still here — that was if he was still breathing. I knew that he had to be.

~

Rude Boy

STEPPING OUT OF MY BEDROOM, I made my way down to the first floor of my home. My team was all present, and the last-minute request to show up for a meeting was the last thing on my mind. I had to ensure I could balance killing these muthafuckas and leaving for good. It was no use in leveling these options of playing in the business or just walking away with my life, and the last thing Shanti told me was we had enough to buy us a paradise. She was happy and wanted to feel unchained from the thought of ever having to depart because of our illegitimate lifestyle. It was time for me to show my pain for her. I was ready to bathe in the blood of every enemy I had knowledge of.

"It's about time you woke up, man; we've been down here since nine o'clock. All the expenses and profit for the pay in. What's new, and where the fuck is Daffy?" Cinco stood up to his feet.

"How the fuck should I know? I thought that was the reason we were all meeting. I don't have time for that shit. Right now, we need to be figuring out how we're about to pave our way out this bitch. I don't know about y'all, but all this shit we making ain't meaning nothing if we ain't expanding." I pointed at all the bags of money I had sitting on the table.

"And you say that to say what?" Bonnie butted in.

"I say that to say we might be packing it up soon. I want that fuck nigga, Polar's head. That's if Lo doesn't give me what I'm asking. I'm tired of Atlanta, and this city is slowly burning to a demise. This was the final straw when he touched Shanti; I don't have any more room for rules, neither am I negotiating."

"What do you mean, Rude Boy? So, what the hell are we all supposed to do, just shack up and leave all of our family behind? We still have lives, you know?" Bonnie said.

I folded my arms, looking at all of them. Out of all my shooters and head wolves, Daffy was the only one not here. The nigga stayed in his feelings so much that I was getting tired of it affecting the business. He would flip out at the wrong times, and he was the strongest hitta I had mentally — or at least I thought so.

"Look, we've been building this empire since we started to make a name in this city. We know everything about each other, and I wouldn't have nothing if it wasn't for y'all, ya hear me? We've made so much; we've pulled up in more than just down south. I'm only saying that I support you all on whatever you want to do. If y'all still wanna make more money than y'all ever made before and building this shit to a real family, I need y'all right now. I've never been good with begging, but all I can do is ask."

"Bru, you sound like a Kiss Squad member. We here, point blank period, with or without any of that included. This shit right now is bigger on our hands, my guy. Shit, they stopping my bread from coming in with all this beef up alert ass shit. What exactly are we doing here?" Cinco asked, obviously feeling a little aggravated.

Before I could answer his question, my phone began to ring. I answered it quickly, so I wouldn't have to get sidetracked from the task we had at hand already.

"Hello?"

"Rude Boy, this is Lo's assistant from City Hall. This call is to inform you that an act of war has been waged against you for the murder of Beans in District 10. How do you plea?"

I looked at the phone crazy, thinking they must have mistaken me with another leader or something. The disrespect for the accusation alone was more than too much, especially after the murder of Shanti still hadn't been addressed. I was fed up with the bullshit, and truthfully, I was ready to go head-to-head with this cat, Lo; it seemed like it would be the only result into me getting some answers about my woman. Let alone the accusations of killing a person that was helping me eat.

"I don't give a fuck what Lo thinks, I didn't touch Beans. Everyone and their mama know that boy is off limits, and he's helping accumulate paper. I don't know if this is a joke, but I can tell you this. Tell Lo to have my sit-down about my wife being slain in District 10, or I'll make sure that all of this ends immediately. No one have room to do anything. That's my first and last warning." I spoke back through the receiver.

"Your message will be delivered, and the investigation of this matter will take approximately three days. If you are found guilty, the proceeding of your district being wiped out will begin. Thanks."

"Fuck you!" I hung up the phone, sticking it in my pocket.

"Who the fuck was that?" Cinco asked me with a confused face.

"It was City Hall from Lo's office. They saying we under investigation for the murder of Beans."

"What? Somebody killed Beans? That's impossible; I was just around him two days ago," Bonnie said with a nervous face. "What if Polar and them did this?"

"I don't know. All I do see is something weird is going on, and I'm not about to stop mashing the gas until I end it all. The room for beefing with another district isn't what we needed, but before these niggas think they can run anything on this crew, I'll bring this entire city down."

"This doesn't look good at all, Rude. We need to lay low, so none of this stuff blows up in our face. Fighting for Shanti was the mission, but now, it looks like we're fighting against the entire city, and we're gonna lose."

"I'll never lose to a bunch of slime ass people like Lo or Polar. I'm setting the record straight, and I might have a few people that can assist us with ending this for good. I'm only doing what I feel is best for us, and right now, we need all the assistance that we can get."

"So, back to what I was saying, my guy. What are we doing now?" Cinco asked, looking for a definite answer.

"Bonnie can stay here for the night and handle all the last payments from our remaining hustlers. Me, JoJo, and Cinco will make this trip to California to meet up with some resources the Cubans linked me in with. His name is Seven; he's a powerful, political figure out in Oakland, California. I think he'll be able to pull some strings for us if I can get him to understand what we up against."

Just as I said my last statement, the sound of guns releasing startled us all, forcing everyone to hit the floor. Glass shattered, and the sound of bullets ricocheting across my walls forced me to keep my head down. JoJo pulled his gun and fired in the direction of the front door where the shots began, but I was lost in thought as to who in the fuck had enough guts to pull up in my district and crank up a gun battle right in my own yard. I knew that the gloves were off, but this alone showed me that more than just Polar was out to get at us. The entire city was literally trying to erase everything that we worked hard to build.

Bloc! Bloc! Bloc! Bloc! Bloc!

Bullets continued to rain inside my living room, and by the time they stopped, the last thing you could hear was the culprits' engines cranking up and pulling off.

"Is everybody good?" I asked, rising off the floor, looking at my entire crew. They all seemed to be okay besides Cinco who sat up, breathing harshly on the floor. Once I looked good enough, I was able to see the bloodstain that was growing on his side.

"Cinco, you good?" I rushed over to him, grabbing a jacket to try and stop his blood from running.

"Yeah, I think so, but I might need to get to a hospital before Jesus pull my ass over at the red light." He winced in pain.

"JoJo, let's get him to the car!" I shouted as we began to lift him.

I didn't know where to start when it came to somebody ambushing where I lived. The respect of the business had gone sour, and it was time to speak with Sami. I couldn't trust anyone, but his help was going to be needed in order to build the team that I needed in order to go at this situation head on.

"Bonnie, I need you to lay low here and keep watch. I'll have a few of the guys come over here in a second to make sure this place is guarded to the max."

"Stay here after all this extra shit has been going on, Rude? You can't just leave me here alone to handle this. I'm not ready," she stressed.

"Listen to me. You got this. There is no such thing as you can't.

Just calm down and focus for me please," I begged to show her the sincerity of her holding me down through this.

"Okay."

"Look, trust me. It's going to be okay. I promise."

JoJo and I carried Cinco out to the car to get him down to the hospital. In the mix of making our way to the nearest medical center, I got a call from Sami; it was like he was reading my mind.

I let the call ring for a second before I answered. "Hello?"

"You have twenty minutes to get down here, no longer." He spoke through the speaker.

"I'll be there in ten." I ended the call and mashed the gas on my two door McLaren.

~

Polar

IT HAD JUST BEEN at least thirty minutes ago when we commenced with the raid of Rude's duck-off spot, we knew that even this was against Chaos City rules, but the boss didn't give a damn at the moment. I didn't like the pressure being put upon me to step out of the boundaries and guard lines, but the Kiss Squad was on a demon time fast at the moment, and the thought of it calming down was nowhere in the vicinity. In my head, I wanted to tell the boss about this bitch, Shanti, still being in my basement, still being alive. It was too much of a risk, and I wasn't at the point where I wanted war with my own team.

Sliding back into the parking lot of our hideout, I made my way out of the car with Tizo and Joker beside me. They had put in so much work in the past few days that it was unclear to them exactly what I had at hand. I didn't want to inform anyone of my plots and thoughts, but it seemed like as the days just went on, more things were becoming evident.

When we stepped through the garage door that was connected to my basement, I immediately felt my phone ring.

I answered. "Yo?"

"I don't think that's the proper way to address someone involving business, Polar. I'll be short because this is only a briefing." I heard Lo's voice come through the line.

"Oh, yes, sir. I didn't know this was you, Lo. My apologies. What did you need to inform me of?" I exhaled, not trying to snap.

"It's been brought to my attention that the recent attack on my district worker, Beans, may also have something to do with your Kiss Squad. The Wolf crew has also been informed. This matter is under investigation, and if we happen to find out that your crew played any part in this, we will terminate your leadership and destroy your district. Now, the only reason I am calling personally is because of the fact that District 10 has been a nice business friend when it comes to dues and taking care of problems, but in this particular situation, you might be involved as the problem. So, to say that I hope that all is well on your end because we all know that I will handle each and every problem that becomes a problem for me."

"Understood."

"Good, hope to keep doing business after these three days of investigation is over."

"Likewise," I said before hanging up the phone.

I thought to myself about the critical damage this could cause to the squad, and having a full threat come from the boss of the city meant that I had to alert my boss on what was at stake. I still refused, and before I looked weak for Lo or Rude Boy, I was going to go out in style.

"Fuck that. We going out tonight, y'all. Whatever club on me." I looked down at the outfit I was wearing — a $2,500 pair of black Tom Ford boots, an $890 pair of Dior men's jeans, and an all-black Banana Republic suede shirt. I was already looking like I was about to step into a fashion show. I wanted to enjoy this time and money while I had the chance before any nonsense occurred.

"We just came back from pulling a whole mission. You really think we need to be swerving out there in public like that, especially at night?"

"Nigga, this the Kiss Squad. We don't care about all that shit. We either rocking out or we copping out, and that was not on the agenda whenever I became the leader of this district for the boss. We do what we want. Now, I said we going out," I said with authority.

Instead of saying anything against what I was referring to, they all shrugged, and we quickly gathered ourselves to head out. Truly, my mind was on the same thing. I didn't want to worry about retaliation coming from Rude Boy's side; it was the reason I tried to handle things with them smoothly and sufficiently. I needed him gone, and it didn't matter what I felt; it was all just business. I didn't care if anyone else won. I didn't care about the other side getting a fair chance. I just needed to win. Period.

CHAPTER NINE

Rude Boy
Ellery's

Stepping out of my car, I buttoned up my Rick Owens trench coat, making sure my pistol was close at hand just in case. JoJo, my loyal shooter, was right beside me as usual. We didn't know exactly how this plan was going to turn out, but we needed to know. I needed to solve this for Shanti.

Walking through the glass doors, the first eyes that we met were the Cubans that JoJo had his encounter with a few days back. He was already looking like he was remembering the incident, and I didn't need the situation to become even more harmful than what we were already facing. JoJo gave a discreet look to all the men in the room and continued to follow beside me. The sound of piano music could be heard playing by the bar. I noticed that Sami was holding the seat at a table. His face was blank, and he looked as if he didn't have any words for me. Stepping closer toward the bar, I recognized that it was Kamo playing the instrument. He looked as if he was engaged in his own world with the music and didn't look back at me until he finished the tune.

"It is good to finally see you, Rude Boy. I mean after so much support, so much business, so much blood… I can actually say it's an honor to meet you. Unfortunately, I don't like being drug halfway around the country just to come meet with you for a request. We all have requests these days, I guess, but this situation must be serious if I'm sitting way over here in the middle of the fucking ghetto. Can you please tell me why am I here?"

"Kamo, please believe me that it wasn't my intentions to drag you out this way and I must say it is an honor to meet you. There is something much bigger going on than business. There's something much bigger going on than respect. Shanti is dead. I know it may not mean much to the most, but you also knew Shanti even when she was a child. She was taken away, slain with no answers, and Lo is the primary suspect in my eyes. Chaos City has gotten out of order. I need help if I wanna answer back. I won't be able to win this alone, and you, out of everyone, knows the background when it comes to this man. He's crossed you out as well, Kamo. I need your help to make shit even. You're my last option."

He sat his back against the piano and stared at me for a slight second. Unfolding his arm, he laughed at me. "I'll tell you like this, son. Don't you ever, and when I say ever I mean never, involve me and my past with you. We will never be in the same boat. I'll help you. And in return, you gonna help me."

"Whatever you want, Kamo. I'm listening."

"I have a nephew out in California. He's a very sufficient nephew. I mean, well, he's good enough to get the job done. Just so happen that he has beef with the same guy. No, my nephew is not the ordinary dude, so don't waste this time. I'll make sure you stay down here and help you along the way until this is over. And that's just for the sake of Shanti and her dear mother. I can only imagine how she's feeling right now. Once this is over, you repay me by staying the fuck away from me. Shanti was like a relative, and she died in your hands, under the safety of you. What was the need of you? The only way you can fix this is kill everyone and take this town for yourself or else you're gonna slowly but surely drown in your own defeat. My nephew will be in contact. You don't have to worry. He'll find you. Just try and do yourself a favor and straighten your familia."

"I will even if I die trying." I gave him a look of seriousness.

Nodding my head at JoJo, we turned for the door to leave. Once we got to the car, I looked him in the eyes.

"We need to shake up a few things. One way or the other, I'm gonna see Lo face to face, and when I do, I'm gonna kill 'em myself. Make sure my aunt, Jane, is straight. Just check on her. Grab a few of the team from District 3 and let's see if we can make these mutha-fuckas come outside."

"Understood."

We climbed inside, and the song, *Never Know,* from the rapper, 6lack, came through the speakers.

I don't fear no man or no object,

I'ma fighter, I been working on my side step.

They say preparation put you through the process

Look at all the progress…

I didn't have nobody there, so I had to tell myself when to goo!

If I was waiting on you to tell me, I would never know

His words numbed my spirit even more because I truly didn't even give a fuck about what I was up against anymore. I just wanted clarity. I would never be able to live with the fact that Shanti was gone. So, Lo and Polar were going to have to deal with me until I was gone.

Polar

Danielle was bouncing on my dick like a real cowgirl, and I nearly exploded in her guts each time she came down on me. I had that ass all greased up from the titties on down, and she didn't hesitate to take every inch of what I was offering, letting that freaky shit run out.

I slapped her ass, forcing her to go harder.

"Damnnn, Po!" she squealed out.

Lifting her up, I sat her on all fours and pulled her ass up high in the air.

"Spread Daddy pussy," I grunted, sliding back in her milky walls. She was spitting out her sweet passion over my pole, and I was loving it.

Using both my hands to open her up, her wet camel toe cried out to me. I pulled out, put my face at her entrance, and made sure to lick her from top to bottom, tasting all she had to offer before returning inside her. I landed each stroke deep and slow. Her pussy sounded off in delight with each thrust I gave.

"Damnnn, you deeepp!" she moaned out, biting on the pillow in front of her.

"I'm in that shit… huh?" I cupped the bottom of her stomach, sliding in harder.

Her creaming was like music to my ears. My house was quiet. It was secured, and the only sound running through my home was Danielle cumming on me.

Wrapping one hand under her shoulder, I banged her out the real porn way until I nutted deep inside of her.

"Goddamn, Po," she huffed before falling down on the bed.

"I know that's right. I know you aren't tired already?" I grabbed her ass.

"Boy, please. Tired? Nigga, I feel like I'm already sleep." She grabbed her clothes and headed for the bathroom.

I laughed, tossing on my joggers and t-shirt. It was early in the a.m., so it was usually time to link up with all my plays and sell as much fucking drugs as I could. Business was slowing, and the beef had been going a little too viral in the past weeks with Rude Boy and his team. I still held Shanti, and my mind was still made up on keeping her with me. I wanted to be king, and I deserved to be. Even my boss was not a factor in my mind at the moment. I was good as dead if they figured me out anyway, and that was why I made up my mind to slide in and take it all.

Word in the streets was that Rude had it out for me and my squad.

He was creating fire about this bitch and wouldn't even consider if she was dead or not. Regardless, my team and allies were building by the day. I had District 9, which was most of the Mexican cartel, ready to step with me, and I knew I had the entire District 10, which was the biggest and the deadliest territory inside the city at the time. I didn't have shit to lose.

Making my way to my kitchen, my phone vibrated. I looked down at the screen, and it was a text from the boss. I sat it down on the counter and took a deep breath. It was hard to make a decision on crossing out close ones with this whole ordeal, but I was left with no option.

"Alright, boy. I guess I'll be back after I get off from work. At least it'll give me a chance to let my coochie breathe." Danielle came and kissed me before heading for the door.

"It's all good. I gotcha when you off again. You can bet that." I laughed as she walked out the door.

As the house grew silent with me in my own thoughts for a second, the loud explosion outside of my home rocked the walls and shattered every window in my living room. It nearly knocked me off my feet, and it took a second for me to realize what was going on.

Running for the front door. I opened it up and witnessed Danielle's car scattered to pieces on fire. Smoke engulfed the air, and there was no sign of life as far as my eyes could see.

I rushed toward the scene and rubbed my hands through my head. A bitch really had the nerve to bring the war to my home, and I wouldn't doubt for a second that it was just retribution for Rude, and he was speaking it clear.

I immediately jumped on my phone to make a few calls. A lame could make me stumble, but I was the nastiest when it came to playing this game. I had no heart. Now, I was finna show it.

Taki

.   .   .

It was a little bit after 1:30 when I arrived home to Rude Boy sitting in my living room. He was fully dressed in an all-white Balenciaga sweatsuit. His gun was on his lap, but his head was laid back against the couch with his eyes closed.

"Boy, I could of shot you." I locked the door behind me and turned around to look at him.

"I'm sorry. You know I gotta come through here unnoticed. I don't want to draw any heat to where you rest your head."

"Nigga, how many times do I have to tell you aren't no harm to me? If anything, I'll be the one to act bad when somebody sliding up through here. You have to relax, Rude." I tossed my coat to the side and sat next to him on the couch.

"It ain't that easy." He rolled his eyes over to look at me.

"Lo is accepting your request; he's gonna be the final decision on the date, so you have leverage here. Him not dodging you and sitting back waiting until he initiate the sit-down is well enough reason to see what he does. It's going to work in your favor." I grabbed his cheek, kissing him on the side of his face.

He tried to slightly brush off of me, and I straddled his lap.

"You need to relax; you have to ease your mind, and I'm not gonna see you walk around here down and can't change nun." I started to unbuckle his belt.

"Taki, now come on with all this." He struggled with me for a second until I wrapped my hands around his dick. I squeezed and began to massage it until it stiffened in my hand.

He looked at me with guilt and fear in his eyes and quickly bent me over the couch. Pulling down my pants, my ass jiggled in anticipation. He rubbed my plump pussy, and I immediately became drenched from his touch. Before I could take a deep breath, he was sliding deep in me, touching the bottom of my shit.

"Oh, shittt!" I threw my head back in satisfaction.

He didn't hesitate to slam inside me, and I nearly cried as I came hard. He latched on to me and beat my kitty down for like thirty seconds and just stopped.

"What's wrong?" I was panting, wishing that he kept going.

"I can't do this; this isn't right." He rushed to pull up his clothes.

"Are you serious? You're really gonna have regrets with me when I've given you my all. You have to accept the fact that Shanti is dead, Rude. You're gonna run around here and make yourself weak." I hopped to my feet and moved to the bathroom.

Jumping in the shower, anger flowed through my heart and mind. I was so good to everyone else's needs besides my own. One way or the other, Rude Boy was going to see that no other woman was good enough for him.

After bathing and rinsing off, I hopped out and saw that Rude Boy had left as I suspected he would. He was playing hardball in a field that wasn't going to lose. I wanted to see him win in every way, but it would be impossible without me standing beside him.

CHAPTER TEN

Daffy

It had been a few days since I had shown my face on the scene, and even though it was hard for my own beliefs, I stood on every decision I made.

Pulling into Washington Circle, I parked my car and stepped out. Ten Kiss Squad niggas stared me down, obviously clueless to the fact that I was invited. They eyed me until I reached the porch door of my destination.

"Wrong district, dawg," one of the goons said out loud.

I didn't even fix my mouth to argue; I knew what I had at stake. I was preparing myself for whatever I needed to do to become number one. Everybody didn't have the guts to be number one. I was just one of the ones who didn't care about stepping out of boundaries to get what I needed and what I wanted. Plus, I would do whatever necessary. After the past few years of trailing behind Rude Boy, I grew past being the average working assistant. I wanted more.

"My boy, Daffy. I gotta truly say this is a surprise, my nigga. And I know you ain't came all this way for nothing. Let's sit down and talk." Polar invited me in.

People lounged about, bagging up narcotics and counting money. It was one house of money business and operations. I loved the entire feeling I had for the game. I was bred from a different cloth, so adapting to undermining was not in my league. Truth was, I wanted the money and position Rude was in. He just wasn't fit under pressure to deal with anything, and I knew what I could do if that weight was in my living hands. It would be beautiful.

"Nah, I didn't come all this way for no reason, but I'm sure that we'll straighten all that out while I'm here. I'll just get straight to the point, Polar. I want the district for myself. We all know that I've been loyal more than loyal. But it's time to take what's owed to me."

"And you've got living reasons to feel like that, my man. All of that is necessary in the field that we play in. And, trust me, I'm feeling you but, in the end, you came to the Kiss Squad for more than just help. You want to be a boss, and bosses don't shadow behind no nigga. The rules in my book just changed. Rude Boy needs to be removed from the districts period, and it wouldn't matter how; it just needs to be done. The money is always key, but it's more to the story when you have a legacy. You leave with the name you engraved, and, if that story is weak, the stream of your status will fade. I respect what you're doing just from a visual standpoint, but what's next?"

"And what do I get and stand at for doing this? We all know Rude Boy got the head tight now in Atlantastan, and you even know the Kiss Squad can't just trim around his way without someone feeling his heat. Killing this nigga ain't cheap, so how much you talking and when?"

He nodded, and a few of his gangsters stared at me with hatred, but I knew I was the only way; I wasn't a fool by a longshot.

"Like I said, the quicker the better for me... let's say three weeks tops. And I'll throw in a extra lil piece of territory in District 9 for your help and appreciation; it's the best I got to offer." He held up his hands, waiting for my response.

"It's a deal, but I move how I want to move on this. I don't need none of your squad snaking around while I put this in motion. Let me kill the nigga my way." I held out my hand to shake on the deal.

He smiled with a wicked grin, and I knew that I was doing business with the devil. But that was what it all cost. I needed my spot, and Rude Boy couldn't offer that because he was too busy making himself the light. That shit was on a creep to being buried completely, and I wanted to do the honors.

"Deal." He grabbed my hand, squeezing it tightly.

I turned to walk out and didn't look back one time. I was in this nigga's court, so I had to playthings smooth no matter how bad I wanted to snap against the indirect threats. My mind was focused, and all I had to do was one thing — hit up a few of my people and get this clown out my way.

∾

Rude Boy

I HAD BEEN PLACING things together for the way I was coming at this entire situation. Mr. Yustafa was still being very persistent with me handling this firmly, and I couldn't let my bloodline down, neither could I let my baby, Shanti, down...

I was sitting down in the large studio in my basement where I usually recorded my music, me, and Shanti. We even had tracks together of beautiful music that our minds configured. Her singing with my calm lyrics made us feel like the ultimate team. When we had thoughts on our minds, we would find ourselves in the booth, recording our pain and making love until we washed that shit away. Sometimes, I felt like I just wanted to drop everything and leave all this behind. My backbone was gone, and, without my rider here to ride, it was no point in me even trying to drive. It was only a matter of time before I wrecked out and lost everything else in the process. Shanti wouldn't want that shit.

As the music boomed through my ears and I reminisced about my life, JoJo walked down the steps with six more of my trusted hitmen. He pushed a man in front of him whose head was tied in a garbage bag. His hands were bound, and when they reached the bottom of the steps, he threw him to my feet.

I sat quietly for a second before reaching down and ripping the plastic. His face was bloodied, and knots were covering his head.

"I had a feeling we would end up running into you." I fired up my blunt, looking coldly down into his eyes.

"Mannn… Rude, I ain't in this mix, homie. Beef is beef, but I do not got none to do with this. You know I would never touch your girl, bro," Polar's younger brother, Freeze, begged with fear in his eyes.

He wasn't any more than twenty, and he was a major runner for the Kiss Squad. Polar never let him get a taste of the full life because he was obviously trying to protect him, but knowing the ropes, he found his way into still earning a name at the clubs and lakes throwing yacht parties across the waters. Their team was shipping drugs, women, even cars across the water, and when it came to this little nigga, Freeze, I knew I would find out something that would be valuable to my vengeance.

"We all know your brother had something to do with this, let alone her dying in y'all niggas' district. I want to know who the fuck the boss is; who is Polar moving around for?" I slid the 45 Kimber from my hip, sitting it on my lap.

He sweated and fumbled over his words, looking back and forth between JoJo and the rest of my team. When he took too long to answer, JoJo split his eye with the butt of his gun.

"Damnnn!" he whined with his chest heaving like he would fucking die.

"I would hate to have to kill you on the strength, lil buddy. I just need clarification, more like an understanding before I just go around killing everybody you muthafuckas love and honor. Don't die in vain," I threatened him humbly.

"Man, you know how Polar get down, Rude; he hate you just as much as you hate him. That's not gonna make me lie on him about something I don't know is true or not. People can say all kind of shit; that don't mean it's not true," he spat the blood in his mouth on the floor.

"Cool. Well, I guess I'll keep you in confinement and wait until you can remember something." I stood to my feet.

"Bro… wh-you can't do this, Rude; I ain't broke no rules of this city."

The statement alone made my flesh crawl with more anger.

"I can't do what?! This is Atlantastan, nigga. The only place where you can die for free."

Before they could even carry him any further, I walked over to him and placed a bullet between his eyes.

Boc!

The brain fragments of his head scattered across the wall, and his lifeless body dropped down like a bag of sand. I took a look at my soldiers and knew that I had overstepped a boundary that I truly didn't need to cross at the moment, but I truly didn't give a fuck.

"Somebody's gonna die every day until I catch the blood clot that did this to my lady! Ya understand! Fuck Polar, fuck Lo, it's all free game for whoever want to play pussy boy. I say we do whatever we please until we sniff out our suspects. When we do, we eat; I don't give a fuck about Lo's word."

"What about now, Rude? If we make a move right now, we could have the entire city against our district; we can't force that right now. Linking our outside connection is the best way to build this power for what we're up against. We're gonna need it." JoJo looked at me, giving sincere advice.

I thought about what he proposed, and, truthfully, he was right. We didn't have enough stronghold, we wasn't strong enough to beat the entire city, but my ties was the last option I could hope on ripping down Atlantastan and taking it for my own. In order to accomplish that, I was going to cross pockets with every source I could and show this pussy ass white boy, Lo, exactly what it took to fight from my lowest. Shanti was killed behind this slime ass dictator, and I needed my blood back. The easy or hard way.

"Check on all these spots. I want everything paused until a later time. We need all the steppers we can get cause after these few lock-ins with my new partners, we will be plugged around nearly sixty percent of the world."

Not only were the businesses running smoothly and bringing in large income, I already held a title for my violence when I first touched Atlanta, and I made sure I kept that attitude each time I treaded around these streets.

"Check on my people, JoJo. After that, we stepping to meet some important people."

"Understood," he said as the rest of my young shooters carried Freeze's dead body out of my studio.

I turned back around toward my laptop and took my seat in the chair, thinking about a point where I had Shanti just back in my grasp for one last time. It was like my game was immaculate with her beside me. She was the swagger to my hustle, and I needed her like a human needed a spine. Nothing could ever replace that effect.

I fired back up the Backwood that was sitting in my ashtray. Turning back on our song, I nodded my head at what I recently had, and the feeling to make everybody feel that pain started to flow through my veins.

~

Taki
Twenty-four Hours Later
Beverly Hills, California

AFTER RUDE BOY called me last night and told me what his next play was, I agreed to help him with making sure we grabbed some good assistance with this war since we were traveling all the way to California. For a lot of people that didn't understand, our city of Atlanta was tarnished, and demons roamed around daily causing more harm as the days went by. As long as people continued embracing the life of committing crimes, the more it would be a virus with how we destroyed the city as a whole. Rude Boy hadn't said much to me since the other night where I started to fuck his brains out. I couldn't believe he walked out on me for being so lost about this bitch, Shanti. It just took everything in me not to snap. It may seem like it was the kindest thing to do in his head for his loyalty toward this bitch, but when it came to me, it shouldn't never feel any different. I felt disgusting and like a whore when he slid out of my pussy and left me looking stupid in my house by myself. Still, in all, I was moving beside this bastard like a whole idiot.

After we arrived in Cali and got off our private G5 jet, we headed straight for the bulletproof Cadillac trucks that awaited us in the front of the airport. We drove a good distance to get to our destination, but, once we reached the boat dock on the ocean, I straightened up my posture immediately. JoJo and Rude Boy were beside me, so I knew that I would have all the necessary things to make sure shit was not misunderstood. Not only would this put bread in my pocket, but it was going to ensure my victory over this whole ordeal.

When the car stopped and we parked, I looked over at Rude and JoJo, nodding, and we got out on one pace. We wasted no time walking the small distance toward the boat and immediately started to walk up the neatly plated ramp leading to the inside of the beautiful masterpiece.

Waiters and waitresses moved around elegantly, serving anticipating customers. Not only was it a new five-star restaurant, but it was on a 210-foot yacht, just drifting above the water.

"Listen, if we lock in this dude, we gain more than just some product to sell around the city. We gain reassurance and security. We're in this shit for the long run, and securing this spot places us in the lead," Rude Boy mentioned to both of us as we made our way toward the dining area of the boat. Numerous tables were filled with obviously important people, just judging from their apparel and jewelry that dangled around their hands, wrists, and necks. I had my own agenda, and that was locking in on the faces that were making all this happen because my mind was officially made up on where I stood in this game. I wanted everything I wanted and was not settling for any different any longer. Until then, I was still willing to play my position beside Rude Boy until the day I died, especially if he asked me to.

"Got to be some hell of a dude if we way out here in goddamn Cali on a boat. This shit is actually nice; maybe we need to start taking more vacations," I voiced, looking around at all the elegant paintings and expensive food.

Rude Boy shook his head, and I could see the funny expression on his face from my peripheral. He was holding in so many feelings that he didn't know what to do with himself. Business was also business, so instead of me worrying about how I was going to be his one way or the other, I was pushing to see this avenue open up.

Getting to a large room where a few guests sat at the table, I watched Rude Boy walk up to shake a young buck's hand. He was medium built with wavy hair and dressed in a dark blue Brioni turtleneck and a pair of Gucci pants. His feet sported a pair of thousand-dollar Santoni dress shoes, so I knew this dude had to be somebody having some type of pull.

"Rude, I hope the trip wasn't too much on short notice. I'm not a runner when it comes to jumping in shit, so if I don't know the background on what I'm getting into, I don't even waste my time leaving Cali," he said while shaking Rude's hand.

"First off, I wanna say I just respect you meeting up with us on such a late notice. My business down in Atlantastan is crucial, and no, I definitely didn't come this far to have to complain about all the shit that don't matter cause it's pointless. I'm quite sure you have an understanding of what's at stake when involving this individual, Lo. He runs the town so far, and he's pushing his weight around heavy."

"And you plan to take him out is my guess?" he replied back quickly.

"Whatever it takes. My girl was killed in the mix about this dude, so I can most definitely say it's personal, but business is what it's gonna stand on, principle." Rude Boy shrugged his shoulders.

I watched the armed guards that stood around watching us like hounds. We were, as I said, safely secured, but I was still uncomfortable.

This dude eventually sat us down and took a sip of the drink that was in front of him.

"Like I said, I usually never step out my boundaries, but for this case, I don't think I mind. I would like to let you know that we aren't going against an ordinary man. We aren't just going against one man. We're going against the leader of the entire state of Georgia. That means everybody who's somebody is gonna have a word to say if this makes their pockets any smaller than it already is. This isn't a small move."

"And this we do understand, which is why I'm guessing we're here."

"I mean. we're here, but even discussing what's on the plate, how can we guarantee any of this shit will work? Lo isn't just a person you get to. Everybody is looking over his shoulders, even when his eyes are closed. Maybe some thought needs to be placed into what's a stake," I interrupted, bringing them back to reality at who we were speaking on.

"I don't think I recall catching your name. I'm Seven." He reached over the table, extending his hand out.

I stared it down like a filthy dog tongue and looked him square in the eyes.

"I'm no one important. All I know is this business is nothing I want to risk with our lives on the line, so if this is what's going on, I hope you got a heavy team and some major backup." I crossed my legs, looking over to Rude Boy.

The table grew quiet for a second, and Seven smirked to himself.

"I don't know if you guys ever heard of me, but when I come, when you see me, it's clear to see my intentions, and I always expect nothing but the worst for anyone that stands against that. I'll gather my people up in the next day or so, and we'll slide down. I guess I'll be resting under your neck of the woods until this is resolved."

"I mean, I appreciate you, Seven. We're definitely gonna need you as much as we can get, but you don't have to stand until the smoke clear. It's still my situation."

"You can't be understanding me right now. I have my own agenda to settle with Lo from some past pain, and I'm afraid this just gives me the opportunity to even shit out. Like I said, I'll see you in your city in two days," Seven assured before walking off with six different bodyguards.

Rude, JoJo, and I stared each other down at the table. I didn't know what was going to happen next, but I knew that I wasn't about to lose for anybody, even including Rude.

"We're gonna head back home, and we're gonna put this shit in place. I'm ready to get it over with, and we don't need any room for playing. I'm just ready to move on."

CHAPTER ELEVEN

Bonnie

After sitting in Rude Boy's home, I sat back and did a little digging on my own. I did a little research of my own on our new enemy, Lo; his ties with Rude Boy were awkward to me, not only because Rude held the most dangerous team out of Atlanta but the fact that he defeated every organization that came up against them. No law or no other boss had gone against his movements due to what he was capable of. Rude Boy didn't have compassion for much, but he was smart about what he did. Polar wasn't the type to cause unnecessary blood with anyone regardless of him holding weight around Atlantastan. He was more about the money and was sufficient when it came down to making it. Shanti was known in this city, let alone being Rude's wife. She was treated like a queen in the city, and people gave her respect when she stepped through.

Walking around the house, I flicked through a couple of files on Rude Boy's laptop, and my mind started to wander in so many places. Why would Polar be doing this if he was the actual one pulling the stunts against Rude Boy, and why in the hell was Lo disregarding the same laws that he forced us to abide by? The blood rate was up to the steepest in the streets against District 10 and every one that was sticking their nose into the action in the streets were coming up dead. See, over a few years back around 2023, a new district attorney came into office in the Fulton County district. This was back then when gangs and real killers ran the traps and blocks, when they actually had some order about breaking laws in the city. For some reason, this nasty ass district attorney, which happened to be the dirtiest woman in the state, chose to handle all the violence with a major Rico act, which forced all laws to lock up gang members and raid the strength and power of whoever was enforcing the calls. She took kingpins out of their homes and forced people to clash in the turf with everyone switching on each other to stay alive. Not too long after, a major war with the government and the people popped off, and numerous people died. Cops perished under the hands of criminals at their worst. With the city killing each other and the cops dying at a rapid pace, the crime rate boosted by forty percent, taking it up to ninety. No one could breathe wrong without catching a bullet, and it eventually forced them to let the city rotate as it did. The hope was that the people would kill off themselves slowly but, instead, they all snatched their own territory, boosted the guarding like Fort Knox, and dealt open business with specific rules. That was when Lo rose from the grounds and stamped his name by killing anything that vowed to go against what his family and associates set in place. One operation tried to go against everything that he stood on, and they were all hung by their necks from the street poles of Downtown Atlanta.

When the thought hit my head, my mind immediately went to call Rude Boy and give him my view on what was at hand. The shots were not being pushed by Kiss Squad. It wasn't the only crew that played a part with having Shanti murdered for no reason, but Lo was another that wanted Rude out of his way. He had been a threat since the day he stepped into this war zone and had reigned his way to the top of the food chain. Also bringing all of us on his team to a better position was playing the shade, and I was going to prove it.

Before I could dial his number, my eyes rotated to the cameras of the entire home. The sight of four cars bursting through our guard gates forced me to jump up and immediately rush for the guns that set in Rude Boy's guest room. I used my phone to check the camera on the front door and watched as a few of my men outside started to trade gunfire. I lifted the bed and grabbed the first two Glocks that came in my sight. I checked the chambers, placed one on each hip, and grabbed the small carbon 15 semi-automatic. I fumbled with it at first before getting the clip in correctly. My paranoia started to heighten as the sound of gun clamor could be heard just outside Rude's mini mansion. Before I could fully gain my next move in my brain, I heard the front door come crashing in.

Boooooooom!

I rushed out of the room, hanging the assault rifle over the second-floor rail.

Pak! Pak! Pak! Pak! Pak! Pak! Pak!

The gun jumped lightly in my hand as I landed a bullet in the first two idiots that came across the threshold. They immediately started to return fire, and I ducked as the slugs penetrated the walls all around me. I rushed, making my way across the opposite side of the hall to get to Rude's Boy master bedroom. If I could make it to his balcony window, I could slide down the tin pole on the sideline of his room. It was the only option I had, especially since I didn't know how many niggas were shooting their way up in the house.

I ran as quickly as I could and turned to fire the gun again when I heard the footsteps that were trailing quickly behind me.

Pak! Pak! Pak! Pak!

I let off a bundle of shots and watched the assassins cower around the corner before I made my way into Rude Boy's room.

The force of the gun that hit me forced my vision to go blurry, but I refused to lie down. My life was on the line, and the last thing I wanted was to leave without telling Rude Boy the muthafucka to take me out. I stumbled but remained on my feet, rushing toward my attacker blindly. When I felt my arms wrap around them, I clashed to the wall and felt the sharp uppercut to my stomach, snatching my breath instantly.

The next thing I felt was a foot smashing against my jaw. I felt a few of my teeth loosen as I howled in pain. I straightened the dizziness in my head by breathing slowly, and my attacker's face slowly cleared to my vision. When I recognized it was Polar's number one killer, Tizo, my heart literally skipped a beat. I backed up on the floor using my arms, and he slowly trailed in front of me, looming his eyes down on me like a demon from hell.

"Fuck you, bitch! You're breaking city rules, and you know it, Tizo. I'm in the bounds of my home and my district. You buck, and you get placed on the shit list as well. You couldn't kill me if you wanted to." I gained some courage to try and stall him.

He folded his arms with a light chuckle, and the smile quickly faded to a frown before he pulled a black hunting knife from his side.

"I guess we'll have to see, huh?" He tilted his head at me like he was psyching himself out.

My mind knew that I was through. I could hear the other shooters pushing their way into the room slowly, guns drawn. They all surrounded me, staring down quietly before I closed my eyes, preparing to get it over with.

~

Rude Boy
District 13

I HAD TAKEN my time thinking about all that was going to happen in the name of my wife. I had prepared my mind to die with the fact of Shanti's blood on the hands of this corrupted ass city. I was about to make a nigga kill me, or I was going to kill everyone until I ended my mission. However, the outcome coming, I was accepting because I was done playing by any rules. The new connections with Seven not only gave me the extra hand for outside killer support, but the deal he was giving me on the raw cocaine was going to allow me to take over every street, district, or business that was dealing with this shit. It was the purest, and if the surrounding rivals weren't buying from me, we would war if they attempted to even sell a half of gram. It was business, but it was organized business, which every hardball needed sometimes to make shit add up correctly. If a fool didn't agree to respecting my change, they all were about to die and figure it out in the next life.

JoJo and I were back in the city, and after dropping Taki off, we headed to the pad to put some teams together and head out to do some reconstruction wherever we caught it.

I pulled my car onto my street, and the sight of police cars flooding my parking lot caught my sight. I immediately tensed up as JoJo tucked both of our guns on his hip.

"What the fuck is going on?" I said out loud, instantly thinking of Bonnie.

As I pulled into my driveway, a few officers with FBI vests on let me know that it was beyond the small petty police in our town. They barely had enough cops to protect the precinct downtown, and the reinforcement for some flaky ass arrest was going to get shit shaking in a blink.

As I stepped out of my car, JoJo climbed out of the passenger seat beside me. A bundle of cops stepped to the side as a woman with a vest strolled her way past them, making her way over to me.

"Can I ask why the fuck y'all in my yard? This private property. Y'all overstepping and don't forget y'all can die for disrespect like any other nigga in the street."

"You might wanna be meek with your threats, Mr. Bah. I don't think you'll need them after I get my cuffs around your wrists and throw you in the darkest prison on Earth. I guess it's no reason for your introduction being that I know everything about you. Even down to your weed and pill business, your murdering crew members, and your money laundering get-up. I'll be brief, so you don't take this for a joke." She walked closer to me.

JoJo took a huge step forward in front of me, forcing the surrounding Feds to tense up and pull their guns. He was clutching his gun under his shirt, and the situation could have gotten ugly if I wouldn't have raised my hand, forcing him to chill.

"Like I said." She smiled. "We got a call about loud screams from an important citizen, and we loaded up to come and kill a few assholes in this contagious trap they call a city. When we arrived, we found ya shit all shot up, but the sticky part where we stay involved is not your fucking house. It's the dead girl's head that's sitting on your fucking kitchen table like a coaster. Looks like somebody wanted to hurt you bad, but I got news, tough guy. They hurt the wrong girl because her parents are the reason we're gonna lynch and eliminate everybody that was involved. That might start with you," she exhaled with hatred in her eyes.

"That's my fucking friend that you speak on laying in there and alerting me that she's gone only makes this shit sound even worst with you threatening me like I did something fucking wrong."

"The name is Jamiyah Porter, and just to let you know, I'm on your bumper, tail, ass, or whatever you thugs call it. You're under my eyes, and I'm sorry for your friend's loss, but there are closer and bigger people to her that want to know. It's my job to find out."

She walked off on me, leaving me and JoJo speechless on anything to say. I was fuming lava on the inside of my skin, and I was still soaking in the fact of her saying her dead body in this house, referring to Bonnie.

Turning around to get back in my car, JoJo followed, and we got in, backing out the driveway.

"I don't know what the fuck is going on, and I don't care. They stormed my home, and Bonnie is gone; I want war. Now!" I yelled, feeling the sorrow for my soldier losing her life in the mix of this political ass shit.

"Where do you think we need to start, Rude?" JoJo looked at me with all sincerity.

"We suit up and smash on everything that knew the whereabouts of this location. We can knock all this shit down until it falls."

My mind was gone, and I didn't want anything but death. This was what it was built off of, and I was going to bring it to every inch.

Polar

I HAD BEEN PLACING shit in effect, and now was the time to get everything I could up out this shit and burn my way while I was in the lead. I was at war with damn near everybody in my mind, let alone the personal shit I had going that only I knew. After the attack on my girl, Danielle, it sent me to pushing the message for our takeover one way or the other. I knew it would drag Rude Boy out of the grave, and we would eventually have our moment to clash and settle this the Atlantastan way.

It was my daily round up, and I was at the Side bar & grill that set right at the border of my district. A few of my close ones were out, and it was well past midnight. All I could think about was how much fucking dough I would be counting after I muscled my way out all this shit.

When I waved to my hitta, Tizo, that it was time to head out, we moved for the cars, but my motion stopped as I heard the loud noise of motor engines approaching. Not just one either. When the lights came into my view, I recognized that it was at least seventeen cars pulling up to the tip of our border, jumping out of their cars.

I immediately threw a hand up, and the sixty plus niggas behind me pulled every gun in hand like a drumroll. We didn't even hesitate to walk toward the borderline that connected me and District 7 together. It didn't take me a few steps before I realized that it was Rude Boy and his little entourage. They were around the same amount as us, and their guns were just as sufficient as ours. Still in all, we knew it was still guidelines to us spilling the blood first, and nobody wanted to be the first.

"Wassup, bitch nigga?! You give me a reason to say we don't just scream fuck Lo and break the terms now. Seems like we been doing it," he yelled with an AK-47 gripped in his hand.

At least fifteen killers surrounded him, and they all looked as if they were prepared to die. I walked closer to the line, meeting him face to face.

"As much as I hate you and the fact that you have clashed with this other side so much is more of the reason, but I'll say it once and leave it up to you for a decision. I don't have shit to do with whatever beef you holding, don't care what you feel it look like. I'm the horse, and it's my mouth, nigga."

He acted as if he was ready to risk it all and start off our purge earlier before we got a decision. Both sides clutched on guns and weapons, mugging each other down, and if shit got ugly, no one was bound to make it out this shit. We continued to eye each other until the sound of his phone ringing broke the silence. The streets were silent and thick with murder in the wind.

He picked up his phone, saying hello, while still locking eyes with me. He listened to whatever was said and hung up.

"We gotta see each other soon, Polar. It ain't no choice no more. I'll give you some advice. Shoot me in the back as I walk off because the next time I see you, I'm handling it with you for good," he spat before turning away to leave. His crew piled back up in their cars and left cloud smoke in the air as they pulled off recklessly. I knew that he would try to make good on his word. I still held the advantage, and he still didn't know yet.

CHAPTER TWELVE

Lo

As I sipped a glass of gin in my office, the sound of a knock at my door made me look up at Taki, looking more delicious than a delicate treat, walking in. She was swagging her clothes to perfection, and I never knew it was just nothing when I had encounters with her.

I stood to my feet, lighting the cigar that was inside my ashtray.

"Taki, you look pretty nasty today. I think you should keep the style. It fits." I smiled, folding my arms.

"I try to keep a switch on it when I can. Sometimes, I don't know who I may be. But that's another story. I've came for confirmation on the sit-down. Are you granting this meetup or not, Lo?"

I looked at her, pondering, trying to see what she really had on her mind. I wanted to know why she was so infatuated with seeing Rude Boy's victory in this entire ordeal.

"I would really like to know what he does to make you push so hard, darling? Is it the money? Well, that can't be because I pay you quadruple what he's worth just to be pretty and keep important matters in order."

"I think that my business is no importance to anyone, Lo. I've never given you a reason to third degree me before, so you won't make a reason now. Please, if you don't mind, I'd like to get this moving along."

"As well then. We can sit down in forty-eight hours, and I stand clear when I say this. It'll be the last meeting where anyone forces me to explain myself. Make sure that you know where this boy stands when he arrives because we don't tolerate rebellious minds in my vicinity." I puffed on the cigar in my mouth and glared at her.

"All of us are in this game for something when we have a reason. I don't think none of us can make the wrong choice with anything we do, Lo," she said before walking out of my office.

I sat back down, staring out of my office window and contemplating my next extravaganza within my town. We needed space and having too many wanna be kings left room for everyone to eventually wreck the entire chessboard. I had a few problems to resolve, and I was prepared to slaughter as many needed to enforce my word. I ran Atlantastan.

Agent Jamiyah Porter
Federal Bureau Investigation Building

It was almost ten in the morning, and I had been up late at night in the office, catching on some extra leads and things that I needed to know about this Mr. Khalifa Bah aka Rude Boy. I knew that he was highly dangerous and responsible for more than a handful of murders, in and out of state. He was a master manipulator and a high-top criminal organization leader. I had no family records, no education files, no files of doctor records. He had a birth certificate from Jamaica but was brought to the U.S. around a young teen. I didn't know what to start from or where the hell I was going. Just looking in that man's eyes, I knew that he was a heartless animal, but I was on the trail now, and I wasn't letting up.

My superior walking in paused my brain talk, and I tuned in because he never stepped foot in my office for no reason.

"Good morning, sir."

"Porter, good morning. The file for the meeting this afternoon, I need it edited and shot to my desk. Also, you have a patrol call about some scared ass people about the house of death over in the bottom of District 10. I'm sending Lace out with you just for a safe eye. Got it?"

Yes, sir. Crystal… Uhh, Mr. Mason?" I stopped him before he could turn and leave.

"Yeah?"

"I wanted to ask if I was working on taking down someone and following up with a great case to get it done, do you think I could have your backup on being the surveillance to tracking this person myself?"

"Porter, what are you talking about? Who are you speaking on?" he exhaled with exhaustion.

"It's a young, wealthy criminal drug lord that's also spilling blood and life all over the streets. He's a problem, and his name is Khalifa Bah."

Mr. Mason got silent for a second, but his entire energy changed when I mentioned the name.

"Jamiyah, I don't know what you have been devising or what you may have going on personally, but I really think you need to slow down and stay in your place. You're exceeding your power," he stressed.

"What do you mean? Khalifa Bah is the…"

"I don't care about nothing you're researching. Khalifa Bah is a red flag. We are too close, and this individual is surely not new on a couple desks in our field. He's not the average one, neither is the force ready to acquire him just yet. So, the pictures need to stay to a minimum."

"But, sir?"

"Jamiyah, I said no, and I don't need any of your superwoman antics behind this later on after this conversation. Work your way slowly and handle the minor things. That man is far away from the roster and needs to be left alone, Porter," he warned before leaving out of my space.

I huffed with frustration, knowing that he was going to be moving weird and strange, and even after his warning, I still gathered a little more information about my bullseye and quickly made my way to my duty call.

I thought of this soulless reaper needing to face his deeds, and I refused to see him make it out before I broke every spirit bone in his body. We weren't the police; we were the FBI.

~

Taki

RUDE BOY, a few more of his apprentices, and I were ganged up in my living room, waiting for him to think of whatever needed to be said. Getting the confirmation that his sit-down was less than a night and a wake up, he was anxious to get the green light to wreck himself until he was killed. His mind was so gone, he didn't recognize that his birthday had just passed. Shanti had his fucking nose wide open, a dead bitch who couldn't even spread her clit if he asked, and this was the reason he was going all out. I tried everything I could on persuading him to just come with me and leave all the fuck shit in this tacky ass city behind. He mashed all his loyalty into some crews and people and felt that the untouchable range was never to fall when it happened to the best of 'em.

"I know you're probably mad at what I'm doing, but it ain't no other choice right now that I'm being left with. If we don't fight now, we're gonna lose everything we stand on and got. We still ain't even got back for blood for the same dead ones that made it possible for us too. I'll die trying to rebuild this shit. What else do I have to lose?"

"You got a lot to lose, nigga. You can get snatched by them Feds, you can die, you can lose more than just things you love. What about us losing something that we love? What if you lose me?" I shot the remark, knowing that he would feel some form of guilt.

He paced around, and I didn't care if he twisted it a thousand different ways; he was going suicide mode and couldn't shake out that shit. He was falling right for the trap Lo was setting, and if he didn't fulfill my request, then cleaning house and moving on was going to be next.

"We got a day or two to get ready for what I'm speeding towards, and I feel like if we get the head start, our chances will spark way harder. Tell me that I'm wrong for wanting my peace. Cause we'll never be able to relax again as long as this shit is over us."

"I don't know, Rude Boy; I guess you're right. If it makes you feel great and not care for anybody else thoughts, prepare for a movie."

I knew that he had felt the energy that had been coming from me the past few days, and it was getting rougher by the day. My sweet ass best friend's ways had faded, and lately, it seemed like I was throwing more shade than anything. I knew that Shanti was his love, and I knew that providing for his team was his soft spot, but the lack of support had me second guessing how I was feeling at the moment. I was never a loser of the game, even if they snatched my soul out of me at this exact moment.

"I'm giving everybody the option to tear it down if they want to now. I know shit could switch on any of us at the last minute. I'm handling what a lot of these so call fucking leaders will always be too scared to. I just feel principle is tougher to stand alone and be defeated. before I'm labeled a coward and allowing all we stand to crumble in front of us, I'll stand on it and die," he voiced, stepping out of the living room.

I didn't even think about entertaining his stupidity at the moment. He was pressing for something that didn't even matter, and it was going to explode in his face before he knew what happened.

CHAPTER THIRTEEN

Agent Jamiyah Porter

After my superior ice-grilled me for the question I threw in the air, I gave it some time to mellow in his mind as I made my way to the active scene he ordered us to go check out. My partner, Agent Lace, was sitting quietly in the passenger seat, and from the look on his face, he was tired of the justice life as well. I always felt honored to go and protect my state and country. I was the black widow to the streets, a woman that could show a criminal rules still existed.

Reaching District 10, we made our way in front of the home we were searching for. It was guaranteed a drug port looking at the view of the expensive designs and fancy cars that sat out front. This wasn't the ordinary neighborhood. It may seem innocent and quiet, but it held a group of psychos that gave no thought to anything but themselves. The Kiss Squad territory was heavy in District 10, and it was a location that made me itch just standing around in the vicinity.

"Let's just get this shit over with." Lace shrugged with no care.

"Agreed," I added as we walked up the driveway to the porch.

The windows were all blacked out as if they had a mirror reflector on them. We looked and listened around before knocking firmly on the door three times.

We both glanced at each other, and a still silence fell over us. The locks started to move on the other side, and, seconds later, the door was opened by a young man that looked like trouble. The dreads on his head and the tattoos aligning his face gave that dumb ass clue away.

"Can I help y'all?" he asked, standing behind the door.

"Uh, yeah, good morning. I'm Agent Lace, and this Agent Porter. We're really out here for a routine check. We had a few calls from people saying they've been seeing and experiencing some strange things at this home — like drugs, maybe a little human trafficking, shit, a whole heap damn things. Are you the owner?" my partner filled him in.

I was watching his background intensely. I could see movement behind him as if someone was trying to get out of sight in case we decided to come in. The smell of marijuana and liquor reeked the air from his doorway, and something just didn't seem right.

"Man, you sound goofy as hell, muthafucka. You ain't got no call from this spot; y'all need to beat it. We don't need help with shit around here, ya heard?"

He moved to slam the door, and Lace placed his foot in between, barely catching it.

"Excuse me, my man, we actually weren't finished. I mean, you have nothing to hide, right? This literally won't take more than five minutes." Lace held him at bay.

Before he could reply with a stupid remark, the sound of a woman screaming snatched my eardrums. I immediately snatched my pistol from my hip, pointing it at his face.

"Freeze and back the fuck away from the door, muthafucker!" I yelled.

Lace followed suit, removing his gun. Just when I moved to push the door with my foot, the thug pulled a gun from his waistband. I wasted no time sending his ass home.

Boom! Boom! Boom!

My gun rang out, striking him twice in the chest. Kicking the door open, we both proceeded in, and a bundle of gunfire started to ignite.

Boc! Boc! Boc! Boc! Boc! Boc!

We returned fire and rushed behind the large wall and entertainment center for cover.

"Well, it's just my fucking luck. I die on a day off!" Lace yelled as we ducked from the splitting wood and sheetrock.

"Not the time, Lace!" I leaned my gun around the corner, releasing four shots of my own.

Boom! Boom! Boom!

I tried my best to level my vision and see who the fuck was shooting at us. Bending down, I took a deep breath and placed my visual on one. He fired recklessly, and I quickly aimed my gun, firing one shot into his skull.

Boom!

I took a deep breath and listened to the remaining gunfire. It wasn't anything but one firearm, which meant someone was alone.

Crouching and moving around the corner, I rushed toward the suspect. He appeared back around the corner, and my trigger didn't hesitate to give him everything it had.

Boom! Boom! Boom! Boom! Boom!

I watched his lifeless body fall to the floor and quickly moved to check the rest of the home. Lace covered the bottom, and I scanned the top level. Besides a dead body of another woman in the bedroom covered in plastic, we had two Kiss Squad members dead and a whole bunch of bullshit that was about to stir up the streets.

I immediately called my superior for our backup. Searching the home, we found at least two hundred thousand worth of drugs. The only problem was the screams we heard upon entering. We found a woman's body beaten up pretty badly, and now, my conscience was on the move again. Were we too late to save her? It was always a ditch upon trying to save a life in this wretched city. All I knew was that whatever took place in here, the Kiss Squad was behind it.

"What the fuck is this place, a sacrifice destination for hell or something?" Lace looked around with a confused face. "You heard screams like I did, right?"

"That was the only reason I followed you in. These are some bad son of a bitches to kill a woman while the guys are at the front door," Lace said, looking around at the scene.

I eyed the room suspiciously and started to scan the entire home slowly.

"That's my point. I don't think that was the woman we heard screaming. The girl upstairs is too cold; she's been dead longer than the time we just pulled up to this house." I inspected the crib from top to bottom but came up empty. The severity of what we still had in front of us was still more than serious.

It was about twenty minutes later when our superior, Mr. Mason, pulled up with our backup and a fleet line of agents into the small district. We still had to be aware of what was at stake because certain crews, as the Kiss Squad, would go to war with the authorities as if we were just another enemy.

"So, can anybody tell me how we were sent to check on suspiciousness in the home and end up with four dead bodies?" He walked under the caution tape.

"Well, when we alerted the suspect in the residence of our presence, he started to act weird, and that's when we heard a woman scream from inside. As I pulled my weapon, he revealed a handgun, and it basically went from there. Looks like Kiss Squad members," I informed him as he stared around at the scene.

"Mr. Polar, it's not a surprise to hear his crew involved in anything going on around this city. He has a personal profile for his nastiness, and he's beaten so many cases that the government is tired of trying to slam him. It's the same thing for your other guy. Rude Boy. These guys are not regular dudes walking around this town. They control 76% of the population with their corruption and oaths that it's ripping the sanity out of the earth." He shook his head with a hand on his chin.

"Sir, do you remember when I asked could we just do an order to pick up the two most dangerous threats in the city? The Kiss Squad and the Wolf Gang. They control murder, sir. Right now, it looks like a war bubbling, and it looks big. Everything in the past two months has led back to the two, and I don't think it's about to settle. You have to make the judge sign the order," I voiced to my supervisor with sincerity.

He shook his head again.

"Do you just think it's that easy, Porter? It's not… for all we know, the judge has his hands in the biggest pot in this war zone. It's hard to know who's tied in this mine pit and, if the wrong person is pissed off, we all could be at bigger risks than just losing our jobs."

We all got quiet and bounced around with looks at one another because it was more than true. You could possibly die dealing with these criminals, and everyone acted as if they had nothing to lose. We were fighting a losing battle, but I had no other choice. This was what I stood upon.

"Look, I'm not happy to see people dying either, but we gotta be careful overall. You can do some small trails and see what we get until I get a warrant and arrest indictment. Don't do anything heroic, and we can take these assholes down simply. I need you and Lace to keep your nose open for any sign that these two are committing the pandemonium around this state. If these fuckers even give you a reason to kill them, don't hesitate." He pointed at me before walking over to speak with forensics.

I turned around to look at Lace, and he could tell by my expression that I was about to go deep fishing and reel us in the big one.

"Listen. No. Porter, I know that look. We need to stick with protocol. Being a renegade is what marks us in the bounds of dying, remember?" he begged with exaggeration.

"We got work to do. Let's go." I walked off to get back in my car.

We were two people, but I wouldn't put my life in safer hands than Lace, so I was prepared to clash head-on to place a stop on the corruption. Any means necessary.

CHAPTER FOURTEEN

Shanti

I had been caged inside of this nigga's basement for weeks. I didn't have any clue what he planned to do with me, neither did I know if Rude Boy even knew of my existence anymore. My hair was frizzy, and I hadn't bathed in weeks. I ate the food he gave me because I damn sure wasn't about to starve to death. I wanted out of this shit. I just wanted to go home to my husband; they could have the money, the rep, and whatever else their broke ass spirits wanted to chase.

The pussy ass guard walked into the room, scaring the shit out of me. I made sure to fart every muthafucking chance I got, in case they got any stupid ass ideas of raping me or selling my body to a fucking old man. I knew one thing. I was going to try whatever I had to, so I could make it out of the sticky shit I was stuck in. The first chance I got, I was making a run for this shit.

"Looks like the blood is getting thicker, lil mama; your man out there listening to love blues wanting revenge for ya." He laughed as if it were a joke.

Not even seconds later, Polar walked through the door with a few more of his flunkies behind him.

"I don't know how we bout to shake this shit, but we the squad, nigga. We made killing so simple and, in the next few days, we're gonna have some real heat on our plate; we dirt napping anything come near us, period. Fuck rules, no thinking. Our connections have been moving shaky because they know what's in the air. No one wants to get put on the wrong side. So, don't look for nobody else to be out there in that field but us. Get everybody, bring the whole Kiss out. We giving it to whoever asking," he addressed before cutting his eyes over to me.

He walked over, looking down like he was about to attack me or some shit. I wasn't saying a word, and I could see the frustration on his face. He knew that Rude Boy was out for him.

"You know it's a lot of shit going down all about you. I guess some people just can't let love go. I'm gonna give you a chance to win out of all this. You can leave this nigga. Come with me, live rich, and never worry about who running what cause Kiss Squad still in charge. All you gotta do is tell me his business, where all do he lay, what's he got backing him, and I'll do the rest. You'll be wealthy and never have to worry about security again. If not, both of you are gonna end up under the capital buried alive. It's a losing battle."

I balled up my face and laughed hysterically at him. I was all out of energy, and I knew I looked like hell. I still made his remark seem like the stupidest shit a person could ever speak.

"Some'n funny, bitch?!" he barked like I disrespected him.

"Yeah, yo dead ass, nigga." I giggled with a straight up face.

I could see the pressure build up in his weak ass, and just as I suspected, he landed a hard right fist across my cheekbone. My hearing slightly faded, and I immediately got dizzy. I felt my eyes water, and even through tears, I was able to look back up at him.

"You're gonna die side by side with him," he snarled at me with hate.

"Exactly," I spat before going back silent.

"What you want to do with this bitch?" his hitter, Tizo, asked with wide eyes.

"Leave her be. She's already cooperating and don't even know it. If she don't make him stop, watching her ass die for real will change his whole mindset. We still ahead. We gotta hit hard, and we can't slip. Rude Boy needs to die. Now tell Daffy to do his thing." He smirked at me before walking out the room.

I still stared at my watcher laughing at me as if my position was a game. I stared into his pupils and locked his face in my mind. He was owing to perish ten times harder when it was all over. I needed Rude Boy to get me home, and I knew it would get eliminated.

Please find me, I thought to myself, lowering my head into my lap.

Rude Boy

AFTER JOJO and I came back from handling our business with the local Jamaicans at the reggae bar, it sealed another step and also more great ass reinforcement when it came to handling issues. There were sixty island boys that were ready to dice and murder whatever needed on my behalf, and it was still playing as I needed. I knew that stupid ass nigga, Polar, thought that his press was going to build his armor, but my money and genuineness allowed me to place my voice over every district except 5, which was the Mexican Mafia. They were affiliated with Polar heavy, and the boundary was solidified a couple days back after the head honcho bucked on a hundred grand for my marijuana. I addressed the matter smoothly, and after I saw the left foot they were trying to throw in the mix, I vowed that I would take care of the Eddie Guerrero looking motherfucker myself.

I pulled into my secluded home, and something immediately felt off. My security gate was open, and I didn't hear an alarm period. Driving up the pathway, I parked and got out, guns pulled. I didn't know what was bound to happen at any minute, and I wasn't bout to go out for it today.

JoJo and I scanned the parking lot and spotted a parked BMW 650 parked in the dark. Scoping it thoroughly, we continued inside the house. I reached my living room and exhaled when I saw him posted in my living room as if he was in his own home.

"We try to announce when we come here, bruh. If you ain't notice the big ass security gate, Seven. Why didn't you call?" I relaxed and tossed off my jacket.

Two more people accompanied him. One healthy, black haired, white woman had green eyes, and her clothes were all black. She chewed a piece of bubble gum, staring me up and down, and I noticed the Beretta 9 mounted on her hip.

The other was a slim, Black man with wavy hair. His posture was awkward, and he moved slow as a turtle, sipping whatever that was in the Styrofoam cup he held.

"You mean them cheap ass pieces of wire you got out there. You might as well move. Don't worry though. I got my people hooking you up with some of the best security systems and a little more safety around this bitch because I figured you might need it. We rode around this den a little bit and peeped the energy. They know we here cause we turned heads with every inch our car moved.

"Rude Boy, this is Dahlia; she works with me in Cali, and she handles idiots for a profession. She's my hound and guaranteed to step with us to breeze in and out." He pointed at the enticing white woman.

She blew a kiss and went back to twirling her hair.

"And this right here is my boy, Yazi. He's an expert in accounting, killing, and investing. He's like the shadow of me, and I seemed to move perfectly with them in Cali in whatever war. As you know, we having our stands out west too. It's just as worst."

"I most definitely know and still hate that you had to place this in your time, but it's no room for excuses going on within my family right now, so I'm headfirst, out there for mines anyway. Tomorrow, I have a sit down with this dickhead, Lo. After he grants me my pass, I'm scorching Polar and anybody that stand beside them. I was about to burn their district down with my own two hands and not about to stop until nun of them niggas are breathing."

"Well, I mean, I'm here, so the game plan I guess would be great right now because we still have hundred kilos of business to attend to. How in the fuck do you expect to sell anything if you loading up to jump from space to Earth, my nigga?"

"I have the perfect avenue. The main mission is to smash this opposition and allow our product to chokehold the streets from behind. We rolling with my first ideas, and I want that in place before we sit down. After we take this shit, we rebuild it." I sat back quietly.

"Sounds dangerous. I just came all inside of my pants." Dahlia grinned.

Seven smirked at me, and at that point, I knew I had to handle all I could and get my funeral arrangements ready because I had a batch of nutcases.

∼

Taki

THE DAY HAD FINALLY ARRIVED that Rude Boy had been waiting so eagerly to see. We were heading down to Midtown to have the sit-down and see how this situation would turn out. If the request was granted, chaos was surely about to unfold, and people had yet to see what Rude Boy was actually capable of. Even with his hard hand, the task was life risking as well and was definitely going to leave a stain. It was the reason the city never slowed down because everybody wanted to be ruler. The truth was, nobody ever lasted.

Arriving down to the capital building, I climbed out of the truck, along with Seven and Rude Boy. Our team full of guards was stepping out of the following two trucks, trailing our steps. We were all armed, of course, and it was always a gesture Lo didn't take well, but I guess it was a little too late to think about that.

We entered the building and took the elevator to the third floor. Of course, when we arrived, Lo had his own armed security mounted in front of us. We continued to move until we reached Lo's office.

When we entered, Rude Boy immediately locked eyes with Polar and his crew sitting on the opposite side of the large meeting table. We all moved behind Rude and stood on the other end. The looks were fierce, and Lo gave a tiny smirk as if the face-off amused him.

"Well, it looks like we're all here. Rude Boy, leader of District 7, and Polar, leader of District 10. There is a dispute, and someone has violated the law. We're here to hold justice, we're here to hold law, and we're here to hold order. The matter has been addressed, and this would be the time to place it all on the table. If you have broken rules, you can choose to forfeit your district position and get the hell out of this city. Leave with your life. If not, you battle to the death, and believe me, death will come," Lo huffed, taking a seat.

Rude Boy was the first to speak, looking over into Polar's eyes.

"Business is business, and law has been broken. My wife was murdered in your district, for no reason, no accusation. Rules of Chaos City. No woman or child is subject to be harmed, period. Regardless of district times or issues with enemies. I want blood for her, and you can't back out of what's been done. You're responsible, and I'm holding you accountable. We meet for chaos city day and end this." He spoke calmly without blinking.

"The rumor was spreading back to my attention as well about this woman. Rules are rules, and no district is above the next when it comes down to that. State your position on this and after, I tell you my decision."

"First of all, I don't care to worry about what this guy has going around Atlantastan. Kiss Squad is the trending topic, and beefing isn't what we do as you hear the name. I said we don't got shit to do with that bitch dying. Period. Now, as far as clashing. It ain't my intentions, but if we forced, so be it," Polar responded with his killers looking extra crazy behind him.

Lo smiled, bouncing to his feet.

"Glorious. Now that you both have cried, I have my own set of information about this dilemma. Rude Boy, you have stepped overboard placing deaths in my state without my authority, let alone the leader of another green light. The disrespect is dear, and the even bigger problem is to die for. Five years ago, I lost my sanity, I lost a piece of my blood, and I lost respect from my parents and associates. This was my actions spilling darkness over my operations. My brother was a well taken care of kid, and I came home to my mother distraught about him running away from home. He was intelligent and raised to be elite, so I knew that a mind like his would probably fall into whatever journey they may. That worry lasted five long years. Through my dad and mom's suffering, I've finally found the answer to give them, and you, Rude Boy, has given me that gift. You have something that I want, and, in this case, it's not an option."

"I don't know what the fuck you're talking about," Rude replied harshly.

I got a bad feeling in my stomach listening to Lo speak, and we didn't need shit to get out of hand, not at this moment."

"Oh, but I'm sure you do. See, the long days that my brother has been missing, it comes to life that he has been with you. I love JoJo, practically ten times more than you showed him when he began to work for you. All this time of our worry, and you've held a piece of me under my nose a great amount of time," he stated with a straight expression.

Rude looked so confused and turned to look at me. I couldn't do anything but shrug because the shit was a shocker to me as well. It explained why JoJo dodged his guarding time and volunteered to ready up the crew for whatever Rude decided. He never left his side, but when it came to the capital, he never got a mile within the district.

"How in the fuck would I know something like that? I met the young boy, and he was homeless. I took him in and provided. I had no clue he was a missing relative of my major superior. That's common sense. Don't you think this would have been came up?" Rude sat up straight, and his face said that the news stomped on his mental.

"Maybe true, but that wasn't my job to decide on. My parents' feelings dictate who dies and who rises. They've grown more hatred over these years, and that's another situation that will be addressed, but for starters, I want my brother brought to me in the next week, or I'll flush the city dry. Pronto."

"Clear." Rude gritted his teeth, and I could tell he was thrown for a loop with the new rundown of Lo's surprising statement.

"Now, as far as your end. Polar," he turned his finger slowly, pointing at him, "you and the Kiss Squad has been majorly beneficial to me over the past few years, and even holding law on your status has placed me in great spirits. Unfortunately, the past few months, your crew has broken off a leash and committed pain that always come with a price. Law is law, and you broke it. You have no option when it comes to what happens in this city because the oath explains it all. You are allowed no assistance from any district in this state, neither can you decide when the clash ends. If you go against my laws on what is at stake, you, your crew, your district will be slain and stripped. The violation of the killing cannot go unexcused. I grant Chaos City Day to Rude Boy's district, and it begins by dawn. Happy purging and let the best soldier win. You're all excused and also Rude Boy… my brother. One week. Get it done." He flashed a phony smile.

Polar and his crew had to remain seated until we vacated the property and didn't hesitate to get up and walk out.

"So, what was all that about? Who's his brother?" Seven asked, confused.

"My best stepper. I never knew; he never told me. I don't know what the fuck to think. All I know is we've been cleared, and we can't hesitate. We start slaughtering these bitches by morning, and I want the pressure nonstop. It's time," Rude Boy replied back to him.

I remained quiet, knowing that I couldn't let Polar just be thrashed without a heads up, but the rest was still out of my hand for the time being.

"That sounds like my type of party. I did my research on his ass too. He so slow; he doesn't even recognize me. I bet he will soon enough. Let's snatch some souls, my nigga."

CHAPTER FIFTEEN

Sami

The last of our guests had left the club, and I was just about to lock up and call it a night. My bodyguard and I were running smoothly with our cocaine process and food service. We kept a certain pace and was sure to clean tracks as we moved forward.

Grabbing two shot glasses from the bar, I pulled a bottle of 1956 Irish wine from the cellar. Popping it open, I poured us both a drink and lit my cigar.

"To our fucking success. We've tripled our sales and loaded up connections from every district in this fucking dead land. Soon, we can branch off and make the rules for ourselves. Look what patience gets you, huh?" I chuckled, giving my guy a toast.

"Seriously, Sami, at this rate, who knows what could happen? We play our cards right, and the rest of these dominos will fall. I don't think this city would look too bad with a hint of the West Indies trails flooding the streets," he said.

"The streets are always adapting, and the Cubans will always win.

This little trick up my sleeve is the start, and we can only get bigger from here, baby. On my mother. This shit is in our hands." I smirked, taking another shot.

The sound of the front entrance opening forced me to look up, and my guard immediately pulled his gun when we noticed the fifteen mafia looking men walk inside with Lo directly behind them.

"Put the fucking gun down!" One of the security raised his M-16 assault rifle with no hesitation.

We were outnumbered with guns, and Lo walked over to me and took a seat at the table in front of us. My guard was stripped of his weapon, and a few of the men kept guns drawn to his head in case he even flinched wrong. Lo had never made his presence in my establishment, and if he was here now, it surely couldn't have been good.

"Ohhh, Sami, take a seat for me, will ya?" He pointed to the chair in front of him, and I followed his orders.

He grabbed my drink and quickly tossed it back in one shot.

"Wooo! That's good stuff." He stared at the glass. "I'm so sorry to make the late stop, but you know what they say when business calls, bosses come." He grinned.

"I'm not understanding, Lo. Is there a problem or something that we can help you with?" I asked, trying to see his motive.

"Yes, you can, matter fact. You can tell me first who authorized you to give assistance to District 10's leader, let alone who gave you permission to also push weight for Polar in my city without certification on this operation. It seems like you have caused a bad stumble, and you're playing a game that has burned you up, Sami. I mean, the Cubans are great, but we still agreed to the terms of your people's residence in my city. Nothing moves without going through me. Rude Boy is running rampant, and you've allowed outside sources that you connected him with to terrorize my throne. Anything you can tell me about that?"

I stumbled over my words, caught off guard by his knowledge, but I didn't picture it coming down on me like this. Kamo was my only backup, and he was nowhere in the vicinity to show his face for me.

"I've dealt with them just to expand us, but nothing was intentional or with any ill will. I never knew it was against entertaining any businessman just like myself," I said, trying to play it off.

"Rightttt. Well, I'm sure everyone knows that when something transpires in my town and it causes clashes, I end up losing money and order. I don't allow anybody assistance. That's the motto of our city. It's all for self and the one who stands remains. You've been a snake, and I know all your actions without you even admitting it."

"Lo, I have no dirty thoughts when it comes to you or this city. I just made a way to eat and stay off the radar. What's wrong with that?"

"What's wrong with it is no one received a bypass. You can't stick your nose in business that you have no dealings with, but when you give help or even kind words to a man that has done wrong, you have become a part of his story, and, Sami, that's what you have done."

His words left his lips, and the sound of a gun firing rang through my ears, causing me to jump. One of the men placed a bullet between my guard's eyes, killing him instantly.

"Jesus Christ!" I closed my eyes at the sight.

"Order is order, Sami. We can't let that go unaddressed." He nodded at me before turning around.

Before I could speak my peace, I felt the blade of a knife slam into my throat.

CHAPTER SIXTEEN

Rude Boy

The night had grown late, and my move was set into effect. Me, Seven, JoJo, Dahlia, and Yazi sat in my living room, quiet after discussing the recent problem that Lo explained at the sit-down.

"I just wanna know why you never told me?" I looked over at JoJo sitting in the sofa chair quietly.

"Because I never thought that you would actually clash with him one day. I ran away at sixteen, Rude Boy. When you found me in the streets, I had nothing and was tired of the torture I experienced being a part of their family. I wanted to be free, to be normal, and just live as I pleased. You gave me that, bro. You gave me my conscience to make my own decisions, and that was standing beside you to do what a loyal brother supposed to. I can't go back, Rude; I won't go back. If that means I have to die beside you, I will. This has become my home," he stressed with his fist balled with anger.

I respected his words, and even though it made me furious about finding out, in a way, I kind of understood his position. JoJo was beside me each day since I scooped him up out of the turf. I trained his steps to be the best, and he had shown me nothing but that the entire way.

"Man, fuck that nigga. He don't have to go back around this punk. We can just get rid of his ass and snatch this city up by the neck. Lo is a businessman and a snake. He's out for everyone's defeat as soon as he encounters you. So, JoJo going back will still be a loss. The only way you can beat a muthafucka like that is play by his rules. Be a snake," Seven voiced seriously.

"Death makes every man turn a new leaf," Yazi added humbly.

I knew that we were pondering in the right area and going at it with this man about his own family was a nasty stand, but on the strength of JoJo, I had to stand beside him the same way he had done me.

"We got to move fast and make sure we stick together. If we do this right, we will never have to do it again."

Seven looked over to Dahlia with a wicked smile.

"You're up, baby girl?"

She giggled, grabbed her Alexander McQueen trench coat, and headed for the door.

"See you guys in the play zone." She waved her fingers.

$\sim$

K-Roc
District 10
East Point
10:15 a.m.

I WAS DIGGING deep in this young hoe's pussy like a jack hammer. The lights were still dim in the house, and I was having fun with the sexy lil fling I picked up at the gas station down the street earlier. There was nothing like being with a boss, so when a nigga said move, them hoes ran.

I was slamming in her pussy from the back, watching her juicy ass cheeks clap against my pole. She was wetter than a tongue dripping saliva, and it took everything in me to not make her a part of my family. I stroked her deeply, listening to her cum gush around my dick.

"Give me more!" she moaned lightly, moving her hips harder.

I slapped her ass and pumped harder inside her. She matched my eyes and made sure to throw it back to match my energy.

"Beat that pussyyy! Deeper, Daddy!" she whined as I plunged my manhood lower in her tummy.

"Ahh, fuck!" I grunted and placed both my hands around her juicy, vanilla backside.

We fucked like it was the last day on Earth and just as I felt her cumming again, I exploded inside her guts roughly.

"Shittt!"

I slow stroked her, calmly letting her cream cover my piece before slowly sliding out of her.

Lying back on my bed, I closed my eyes, exhaling from the session. I was damn sure feeling great.

"Oh, no, it ain't no sleeping this morning." She rubbed my chin with a laugh.

I rubbed her thigh, smiling at her nastiness.

"You've drained me, baby. I've got to reboot for all of you."

She kissed my cheek and climbed out of the bed.

"Well, I'll go and fix myself something to drink because you only got thirty minutes, or I'm taking it." She rolled her neck and jumped to her feet.

I didn't bother to reply. At least thirty minutes would let me jump back right with my mojo because I wasn't going out bad with no pussy. My eyes were shut, and I was nearly dozing off when I heard three gunshots ring out.

Boc! Boc! Boc!

I raised up in my bed with my adrenaline rising immediately. I remained still, thinking I might have just been tripping off the edibles, but a quick four more shots blaring out alerted me that I wasn't.

Boc! Boc! Boc! Boc!

I jumped out of the bed and snatched my dresser open. I scrambled for my gun, and it took me a second too long to find it. Grabbing the Ruger pistol, I turned around to my young, white chick standing in the doorway with a 40-caliber pistol. She was grinning from ear to ear, and it didn't give me the vibe of the woman I was just slaying in my bed.

I raised my gun and pulled the trigger. It clicked loudly, but nothing came out. I pulled the trigger again, and it clicked once more.

She walked slowly over to me and peeled the gun from my fingers as I stood frozen in place.

"Your bullets were flushed down the toilet before we fucked, baby. I hate to destroy such good dick, but you have expired." She raised the gun to my head and frowned.

"Who the fuck are you, and why are you here? Do you know who the fuck I am, Mama?" I clenched my jaws.

"Well, my name is Dahlia, but you can call me poison. You're the example; hopefully, you'll be forgiven." She pulled the trigger.

Boom!

~

Rude Boy

TODAY WAS BRIGHT, and I was out for the hunt. I wanted Polar's fucking head, and I wasn't stopping until I did. I had nine soldiers riding with me, three cars deep. All of us were armed enough for a twenty-man army. It was my time, and I was killing these niggas on fucking sight. I was stepping on everyone affiliated and whoever caused my business a slump.

Driving the car through District 5, I stared out of the window while glaring out at the streets. They'd never seen a menace that was willing to risk life to win. I was about to show all of them exactly what I was.

We arrived at a large white home surrounded by a black security gate. I pressed the button and waited for a second before gaining entrance. It slid open, allowing all of my team to enter.

By the time Mendez was walking into the parking lot with his men, JoJo, Seven, the rest of my hitters, and I stepped out, clutching.

"Damn, my friend, you show up all Tony Montana. Have you had breakfast this morning?" He chuckled.

A few of his men laughed along with him, and I didn't even want to waste too much time, so I got straight to it.

"You received product from my people, and you didn't pay. A hundred thousand dollars' worth. I don't see it in your hand, so that's gonna be the wrong answer for what I'm looking for. Also, you've seemed to have sided with Polar as an associate, and you know that we are at odds. It seems like you're pushing your weight and stirring up smoke?" I asked, ready to snap.

"Is this man serious?" He looked around. "First of all, you won't get a dollar from me for anything. Yeah, I'm associated with Polar, and the money I'm making doesn't need you or him, so I could care less. We're Mexican, puta. We can do what we want."

I pulled my gun in a blink, placing one slug in his head.

Boom!

The guns immediately started to flare as both sides broke for cover. Bullets started to fly, and bodies started to quickly drop. Two Mexicans were slaughtered by Seven's Glock 17, and he didn't hesitate to stand over both of them, finishing it off.

Boc! Boc! Boc! Boc! Boc! Boc!

One of my soldier's head directly behind me nearly flew off his shoulders. The bullet nearly knocked his skull out, and I slung my gun recklessly, catching another one in the neck.

Boom!

JoJo stepped in front of me, releasing his AR-15 semi-automatic.

Pak! Pak! Pak! Pak! Pak! Pak! Pak!

I watched three more men fall to their demise from my young shooter. He slowly continued forward, still firing his gun.

The last two Mexicans were struck trying to retreat from the stampede of slugs that riddled the back of their heads and shoulders.

Pakkkk! Pak! Pak! Pak! Pak! Pak!

The gunfire had ceased, and dead people scattered the large parking lot. One of my nine killers was dead, but the message I was pushing was just beginning with these pussies for the disrespect.

I held my gun in front of me as we secured our surroundings. I walked down on Mendez lying on his stomach, breathing harshly with blood rushing from his mouth. I could see he was dying from the large hole through his back.

"Fuc-fu fuck you. You're dead!" he choked over his words with a look of pain written on his face.

"You've made a big mistake and so did the rest of this city going against me. You won't get that chance again, Now, tell Polar to get you into heaven, pussy hole."

Boom! Boom! Boom!

I plugged him with three more bullets to the head.

"We might need to be getting the fuck out of here. It's ten in the morning, and we just did the dash through this bitch!" Seven yelled, moving for the car.

I didn't hesitate either. My crew piled back up in our cars and smashed away from the scene, not having an ounce of regret. I was going to make sure the young kid that stood for my family was good for life and push to get the body for a burial. It was a part of what we did, and it wasn't finished. I wanted all of them dead.

CHAPTER SEVENTEEN

Polar

I had already started getting calls about the massacre Rude Boy was causing around our territory. We had a number of secluded properties, but so much was going on that I didn't want to risk anybody finding out where we rotated because anybody could be working against us.

After the boss had been raging out on me to the most high, I was waiting until they arrived to see what the next move was.

I didn't have to wait too long because not even two minutes later, the boss was walking in with three Kiss Squad hitters. Tizo was posted by her side as usual, and I didn't even want to open my mouth already in the hot seat with the matter. My plans were still set in my head, but I had to tie all knots together.

"This has to be the stupidest shit I've ever seen. It was simple. We were supposed to kill that bitch that night. Not kidnap her, Polar. You've torched an entire fucking war, and Rude is standing off with Lo because of your dumb ass mistake. That was never a part of the plan."

"It's like you don't know what you want to do with this nigga, Taki. Kiss Squad beef with this nigga in the streets, sis. He ain't letting up about this bitch. You wanted her gone regardless," I blurted out, speaking too much.

She snatched her gun from her waist, shoving it in my jaw.

"I started all this muthafucka. I earned every coin, and I built this crew with my own hands. I pay you to handle what I say, not what you feel. Don't ever say my fucking name again and throw the squad in the field to fight and slump the rest of those bitches. I'm not worried about you hurting Rude Boy." She pulled her gun back and quickly texted someone on her phone. "Where in the fuck is that bitch?"

I couldn't cave in like that, and I still had too much at risk.

"I don't know. I left K-Roc with the bitch and told him to get rid of the bitch. That was yesterday," I lied.

"I don't care about what you saying. Find him and I'll see for myself. Clean this shit up now." She turned on her heels, walking out on me.

The shooters that I did have in the room stared around quietly, and I tried my best to quickly get my thoughts together.

"Y'all head out and grab a few more. We don't run from shit, so if we got to lose a few to kill these people, let's do it. Set up patrol around the district and deny all dealings with any other district until this massacre ends."

"We on it, big dawg." One of my hustlers spoke and headed out the house with the rest behind him.

I was nervous as fuck. I just needed to buy a little more time, and I was going to pick up enough money to last me for the rest of my life. I was overdue for the win, and I was snatching Shanti up to join me with a whole new life. Taki was my sister and the boss, but she was my way.

~

Rude Boy

.   .   .

WE HAD BEEN on a rampage throughout the night, and after letting my crew rest for a few hours, I drove around in my district, strategically putting together the next checkmate. I had over four districts backing me with Chaos City, and the Kiss Squad was dropping left and right before the sun could drop. I accepted what came with this game, but that had to be vice-versa on the opposite end because when it started, it wasn't stopping.

I noticed an all-black Dodge Durango behind me not too far, and it only caught my attention because the headlights would pierce my eyes every few seconds. Of course, I was on to it when I first saw the car, so I made a call. JoJo had been following it for about thirty minutes now and recognized that it was the federal bitch. She had a tail on me, and she was lurking around trying to find anything she possibly could to play chess with me. The one thing about me, I was always a step ahead when it came to war, and I didn't need a queen to win.

Pulling inside of the plaza in the West End Mall, I parked and made my way across the street and headed inside my family, Simone's, CD shop. She was also Jamaican, a great spirited woman that had been in my life since we arrived in the States. She was more like an auntie to me. She always gave advice, always told the truth, and always showed me how to have a heart.

"If it isn't baby boy. Now, why ya gon break me heart like this not seeing ya for weeks? It's just not like you." She smiled and pulled me in for a hug.

"I know, Simone. Ya know, trying to get things straight. After Shanti…"

"Me know, son, me know. I don't want ya to explain. I know that if ya could live under me home for seven years, than ya love an old woman like me ya understand." She giggled, grabbing me a soda from her fridge behind the counter. "Are you really okay, Khalifa? Don't lie to me."

I never wanted to place her in the mix with what I did for a living, but it was natural for my name to be ringing deeply in the streets of the same district I ran. It was the same grounds where she walked and slept, so my dealings on the turf could easily surf through the air. I made sure she was good financially and secured on safety. It was the worry that concerned her because she knew I wouldn't lie.

"I'm at it in these hell zones like always, Simone. Nothing has changed, and it may never be change. I'm fighting for a reason, and I have to keep standing through all the bloodshed that's lost on this side."

"Sometimes, ya gots to know when too much blood has been shed, son. Sometimes, ya have to know when to fold and keep what's most valuable to ya than the reputation… life." She tapped my chest with love.

Grabbing her in a hug, I couldn't do anything but agree with her words of wisdom. I would always try my best to implement the knowledge she gave me. I was more than grateful for her love because most couldn't get any with the way the world had been since the pandemic and uprising. It was all for self.

"Thank ya, Auntie. I know ya be worried but rest ya soul. I'll be fine. That's a promise." I slid five thousand dollars into her hand.

"Are you sure because I already know who ya dealing with? I could get the big policeman involved, and that will stop all this," she quickly stressed.

"Nah, Auntie, there no need. I'll handle it like always or die trying. I'll be okay. Promise."

"Ya better, boy, and don't take so long to come see me next time."

I smiled and formed a heart with my hands before leaving out. As soon as I made it back to my car, I watched as the stupid agent drove past me as if she was just unnoticeable. I continued to get inside my car and proceeded in the opposite way. I knew JoJo still had eyes on me, but now, it was time to leave this bitch.

My BMW was more than sufficient when I had to be in time for some shit, so I knew that dusting her piece of shit ass little car would be no sweat.

Mashing down on the gas, I quickly accelerated up to a hundred miles in a few seconds. When my car made it to the end of the street, I shot across the intersection, dodging traffic and sliding straight off on the expressway. When I reached the fast lane, I peeled out a little longer and jumped off two exits down. Taking the street way back to my district, I slid to my smaller home to keep a low profile. After calling JoJo and alerting him where to meet me, I sat back and thought about exactly what I had heard from Ms. Simone. Sometimes, you had to know when to fold if it could depend on you having your life the next day. I didn't want to even think that way, especially after losing Shanti. I had to kill until my soul was able to rest from her being gone. I was on it every hour, and Polar was the main casket I envisioned in my mind as I closed my eyes for a second.

CHAPTER EIGHTEEN

Polar

I t had been three days into this Chaos City Day, and the heat was turning up. I had heard a clash transpired in our district today at the usual place where the Kiss Squad gathered and held our meetings. I was on my way to meet this nigga, Daffy, and find out what the deal was with the half of ticket this idiot was guaranteed if he got rid of this man, and he still had yet to do what was agreed on. Nine squad members died in that rampage at the mall earlier, and the organization that we had was falling.

Stopping in the plaza, I pulled up to where he was parked and jumped out. He looked like he was timid as fuck, and I could tell that his energy was not on what he planned it to be.

"What the fuck happened?" I hopped out, looking around before firing up a cigarette.

He shook his head before exhaling.

"Nigga, them folks pulled up to the house and shot everybody out that muthafucka. They killed everybody standing out that bitch. He saw me out there, and it's like he snapped."

"So, you couldn't get that nigga? How the hell you suppose to handle homie if you can't even stop getting caught down bad with him?"

"Polar, this nigga ain't alone. It's like eight killers riding around with this nigga, and they ain't pulling up normal. That ain't even including JoJo. He's gonna kill anybody that Rude tells him to handle. If the lil one comes, he's gonna flush yo ass. I ain't dying on the strength, stupid ass man. That's why I said do it smart."

"Who the fuck you think you talking to, boy? I placed you in position to even have a shot at being a real boss, so watch your fucking mouth before I shoot yo ass in the fucking mouth." I snatched my gun off the hip and placed it to his face.

He stared at me for a second, but I noticed his vision rotate behind me before he pointed with wide eyes.

I turned around to see three black cars smashing up toward the curb. I didn't have to ask if it was Rude Boy because he was jumping out the first car with his gun blazing.

Boc! Boc! Boc! Boc! Boc! Boc! Boc!

We both ducked and squatted behind the cars in front of us. The other two cars began to chase down the other Kiss squad members that stood around in the parking lot.

I continued to feel his bullets strike the car, and as he walked in closer, I took a deep breath and jumped out to rush him with a bullet to the head. I didn't know how close he had gotten, and before I could raise my gun, he was slapping it from my hand. We instantly went to fighting.

"Wassup, nigga?" I jumped back, squaring up. He moved forward, and I swung. He quickly dodged my hit, landing a two-piece on my jaw. It made me stumble, but I rushed him with all the strength I could, pushing his back against the car. When I realized the gun had fallen from his hand, I made my break and took off for the alleyway in front of me. I was running as fast as I could. Before I could get a good distance, I felt the bullets that started to fly past my head.

Boom! Boom! Boom!

I ducked and didn't hesitate to grab ahold of the fence in front of me. It was about ten feet, and I nearly cleared it with one leap. I damn sure wasn't trying to die by the hands of this bitch ass nigga, Rude. I had to get away.

Crossing the other side, I made my way out to another intersecting street and rushed my way into the corner store, locking it behind me. The owner that I was familiar with immediately rushed over to me.

"Polar, what the fuck happened?" He looked at me nervously.

I closed my eyes, feeling a sharp pain overtake my chest, but my adrenaline was pumping too hard.

"I need a phone and a gun," I replied, looking back out the small door windows into the street.

"Polar, you're bleeding!"

I looked down at my side and noticed the large bloodstain that was starting to soak up around the waistline of my pants.

"Shittt!" I grabbed ahold of it and tried to move. I instantly was about to crumble down to the floor.

The store owner, Emanuel, grabbed ahold of me and walked me behind the counter. We entered a small room, and he placed me down in a leather chair. I noticed the business phone sitting on the table and picked it up. Dialing the boss' number, I sat back and waited for an answer.

"What?"

"Listen, I just had another run in with ya boy, and I don't think it'll be the last one. I'm shot."

"What?! Where are you? Did Rude Boy shoot you?"

"It damn sho wasn't Danny Glover. I need a pickup, but I'll text my location," I replied as Emanuel went to working on my side with gauze and antibiotics.

"I told you to fix this, and you go out and get yourself shot. I should have taken over this a long time ago, but after today, I'll show you. We're on the way," Taki fumed before hanging up in my ear.

I watched this nigga pull out these damn scissors and scalpel and nearly fainted. Closing my eyes, I allowed him to do what was needed to save my life, but I had to rebuild and rethink before I came at this nigga. I wasn't about to die for free, and it was time to put shit on pause until I placed my takeover in effect.

~

Rude Boy
10:29 p.m.

I HAD BEEN at it with the bitch ass nigga, Polar, and today, I finally got a chance to run down on his ass. I made sure he saw my eyes before I tried to kill him, and by the mercy and grace of God, that pussy escaped by an inch. I wasn't sure if I hit 'em or not, but I knew if I did, it would probably mean he was either dying or dead right now. No one understood what I meant when I said that I was going to burn the entire Atlanta down until they either kneeled or died. I felt like my life was gone already, and it was going to take a lot to stop this shit that was at hand. I had tried my best to be rich in spirit, so I could be clear to my purest. Unfortunately, my young one didn't want to commit to going back to his family, so the steam with Lo was slowly stirring, which meant that I had to go ahead and make my move against him while I already knew what JoJo's choice was going to be.

We chopped it up while sitting in the middle of the driveway, and from a distance, we could see a car that slowly pulled inside and drove down at a slow pace. We both removed our pistols because no one knew where this address was. I was ready to kill whoever need, and war could be placed in at any time.

I watched Seven step out the front door, leaning over the porch with his M-16 rifle, glancing out as well. When the car came to a halt, a man stepped out smoothly and closed the driver's door behind him.

He was wearing an Atlanta Hawks snapback, an all-red Moncler outfit, and a pair of black Red Bottoms. I could see the gun that was poking from his waist. He folded his arms, looking at us like we were the ones violating property.

JoJo went to react, and I put a hand on his chest.

"Holdup, who the fuck are you? Cause if you don't know, you won't make it back to that car," I asked in a low tone.

He smirked at us and cut his eye over to Seven standing on the porch with the gun in his hand.

"I'm nobody important to you or your little friends, but I am important to Kamo. I wouldn't be here if he wouldn't of begged me to come assist with a so-called problem. According to him, his brother, Sami, was murdered. That has started a major disturbance. I'm here to make more of a disturbance. I guess you're Rude Boy?"

When I realized who the man was standing in front of me, the respect didn't take long to kick in, and explanations didn't have to be given because I already knew the background of the cold killer standing in my presence, especially after he mentioned Kamo's name.

"Ghost?"

"The one and only." He stepped closer until I could look him square in the eyes.

"Much respect, shotta. Never thought that I would see you running around in these fields; you got everything on lockdown there where I'm at. It's a pleasure."

"I'll always creep these streets. Souls are owed to me, and I'm still getting payback, and my wife, Erica, runs those islands. I'm just her security," he said, speaking the truth.

"So, Kamo sent you? I mean, you don't even know what's going on, like getting drug into my mix right now is a little dysfunctional. Everybody dropping on both sides, and I don't know when the blood will stop."

Ghost leaned against my car and stared at me.

"I'm gonna be straight up. I was born and raised in these streets, and when I say there isn't any situation or person that I have ever seen stand up against us. That blood will stain this grave land until the next life. He sent me down here to push you through whatever you facing, and after what he explained to me that this was about, it shouldn't be any reason you're not trying to murder everybody that has even mentioned a statement against this problem. When you stain the streets, you mark them forever."

I gave him a firm handshake and invited him inside to establish how I would place a tombstone on the entire Kiss Squad and the so-called ruler of this fucking city. We placed together everything I had to offer, and I was preparing to mash the gas to search harder and exterminate the smallest up to the largest.

CHAPTER NINETEEN

Agent Jamiyah Porter
District 7

I t was going on about eleven at night, and I was treading around Rude Boy's area, scoping out all that I could. There wasn't much that I knew about this devil, but I just knew that he was a spiteful and crooked evil that most people couldn't even detect. He had eyes of innocence, but I was sure that there was so much behind them he was hiding. I knew the story of his woman being murdered, and that was one of the only things that softened my emotions on being a super ass cop. That experience for someone that actually loved their woman wholeheartedly and lost them to the dirty ass streets was something I could feel in my own chest. The only thing about it was that I had been doing my investigating on both individuals, and I'd recognized everything that they had in the air from following each other around a few hours throughout the day, and it was clearly something I figured out that started to make me watch even more professionally. Polar and the Kiss Squad were not alone and judging from his weak war tactics and bad decisions of people losing their lives in this trap, I could almost guarantee that it was somebody who was calling the shots because he surely wasn't. I had a few people in mind, but one was more intriguing than all the others. Her soul oozed evil, and you could see that in the recent photos I had, but I couldn't find any major priors against my brand-new suspect. The mode I placed on was finding out what I needed, even if had to do it on my own. My partner, Lace, had taken it home, and I wasn't done on my rampage for solving this case. Turning my car around, I mashed the gas a bit harder and headed toward the borderline of District 10. My instincts never led me wrong, and I had a feeling I was going to catch my bait.

～

Lo
District 1
Downtown Atlanta

STARING out of the massive window of my mother and father's penthouse suite, I looked down at the citizens of Atlantastan and shook my head. They moved around visiting the businesses, the retail stores, and bought drugs from any corner of the station. It was the same fate and gateway to all the other districts, but they were contaminated with narcotics and failure. They were exposed to government enslavement and continued to place themselves in deeper by following the next. It was a major spin wheel that turned everybody in circles. It was truly a circle of life.

My parents coming downstairs for dinner forced me to break my thought process and go take a seat at the table. We had some of the best food in the state prepared by our personal chef, and it was always a great feeling when I had a chance to bond with my family on other notes than just business, but tonight wasn't about business, period.

"Son, you look well. I suppose you are well because you're still alive." My father spoke as soon as I got to the table.

I leaned over, kissing my mother on the cheek and nodding at my old man. He had always been the tough renegade of the family, and it was no wonder we grew up to be the way that we were — business orientated, relentless with accomplishing the most, and never allowing a person not worthy to win at anything they competed with you in. It was more of like a generational motto. Ever since my brother, JoJo, came up missing about four to five years ago, he scorned their hearts with pain, and that fault had been on me since that day. Tonight was the time that I alerted them of the recent news because I had to face this with every breath in my body.

"Yeah, Dad, I am... It's not that easy to take my spirit, but the reason I'm here was for more than just the meal; it's actually not about the meal and spending time at all. I had something to tell the both of you."

My father cut his eyes up at me and slowly sat down his fork. He could see my face was uneasy, but what was on the table would be on it until you made it your business to clear it up.

"What are you speaking on?" He gazed directly over at me as my mother continued to eat.

"A major problem that we have no choice to take care of, sir." I gave him the look while tilting my head toward my mother to be sure we didn't panic her.

He didn't seem to like the gesture, and I could tell he didn't like having to guess anything.

"If this is a normal business problem, just get rid of them, son. It's easy."

"It's not about business, Dad. This is personal, like family personal." I exhaled.

This time, my mom sat down her utensil and looked at me. My father stood to his feet and placed his hands on the table.

"You found out who killed JoJo?" he questioned.

"No, I found the guy that still has JoJo with him right now. He's not dead, Dad. I found him."

I already knew the tears would begin rolling down my mother's face, and her entire energy flipped from soft to horrible. JoJo was her heart, and she hadn't been the same since he'd been gone.

"What did you say?" my father asked me, coming closer to be sure he heard me correctly.

I straightened my suit and repeated myself.

"I said he's alive."

"Are you sure? What source is this coming from, Lowry?" My mom started to grow anxious immediately.

"Do you know where he is?" my father cut in, standing to his feet.

"Not for sure. Wherever he's at, I'll find him." I gave him a look of assurance.

"I don't give a damn who's involved. You kill every last one of those bastards and bring our son home. No excuses."

I didn't even waste my time explaining another thing. I made my way out of their home and headed down through the hotel's lobby.

Making my way to my car, my assistant, Silent, opened the back door of my Cadillac Escalade.

"Is all well, sir?" he mumbled.

"No, it's time, and I want you to make an example. Bring my brother home. Clear the green light on District 7. If he isn't delivered by tomorrow, we burn the zone until we find him."

"Of course," he replied before closing the door behind me.

After leaving my parent's home, I connected all my dots and made sure I unfolded this course in my court. Rude Boy had to be removed. Any means necessary.

Agent Jamiyah Porter

IT WAS GETTING FURTHER into the night after making it to the last scene where I had the last head-on collision with the Kiss Squad. I still had been maneuvering through the property, even though it was shut down after the crime scene took place. I was on their trail heavy, but my mind said that they were hiding more than what it seemed.

I parked my car down the street and tossed the hoodie over my head. The neighborhood was dark, and all you could hear in the background were the signs of aggressive dogs barking in the night.

I reached the parking lot and slowly proceeded up the driveway. I moved along the side of the house and quickly made my way to the back. The house was still in great condition, and a few of the bedroom lights were on, which was unusual because I had been doing surveillance on who was coming and going and there had never been a light on.

The feeling of a barrel being placed to the back of my head sent chills up my spine.

"Police bitch, you thought we ain't been on to you. Fucking with us, you better remember one thing, sweetie. Killing is so simple," he whispered into my ear.

I couldn't even see his face, and all my emotions started flashing through my mind. I wasn't about to stand there and die. Just as I pondered on snapping into my defense mode, the sound of a gun rattled my ears, and I knew that I was dead for sure.

As I continued to blink, frozen in my position, I checked myself to see why I wasn't bleeding. I turned around to see my attacker's brain on the pavement, and Rude Boy holding his gun with the coldest expression I'd ever seen on a criminal.

"Thank yo-you." I shuddered with trembles riding across my skin.

"I should kill you, but I would never sit back and watch these pussies murder you, and I have unsettled business with them. You might wanna stop following me around and reconstruct your job description before you end up hurt," he said, turning to walk off.

"The war between you and Polar is the main objective, Khalifa. The government wants you both. I know that this is behind your wife. That's why you have people that pursue jobs for this. Let me help you," I offered, feeling a good grace for his presence at that moment.

"If you know that this is about my lady, then you know we can't erase that and redraw it. She's gone and so is this city."

"What if I tell you I think she's alive, and I can prove it?" I folded my arms, looking at him seriously.

He stopped and made his way into my personal space.

"What did you say?"

"I said I think your wife is alive, and I can prove it. But you have to help take these bastards down in order to do it."

"Oh, you don't have to worry about these guys, but you will worry and stand on that statement that you just made. Tell me what you know."

"Do we have a deal, Khalifa?" I stood my ground to his demonic ass.

He stared me up and down with his nostrils flaring.

"Deal. Now, how do I find my wife?"

"We need to go somewhere and talk. I'll follow you." I nodded, evaluating the scene of the wasted casualty. Unfortunately, I didn't need any heat coming from Mr. Mason, so I was riding for the gusto, and I was going to bring this disaster to a stop.

CHAPTER TWENTY

Rude Boy

It was early in the morning when I cracked my eyes to the sound of my cell phone ringing. Grabbing it from the dresser. I answered.

"Yeah?"

"I'm glad that you're comfortable, baby. You're so smart about everything that you make the dumbest decisions that are so easy." The voice spoke through the line.

I sat up in my bed, and for some reason, all the sleepiness was washed off me.

"Taki?"

"Who else, Big Daddy? You shot my brother and nearly killed him. Now, the love that I do share for you is starting to split."

I immediately thought about Polar, and tons of flashes started to strike me at once. The way Taki moved around Lo as if she was untouchable. The way of her disappearances and flipping mood swings. The connection was in my face, and I'd never spotted it.

"Your brother? I most definitely tried to kill that bitch, and now that I know he ain't dead, I'll be sure to start back searching, so I can finish what I started."

She laughed through the line, and so much anger was building through me that I wanted to explode. My best friend was a snake, and I deeply knew it and never accepted it.

"Khalifa, you don't realize what is at hand, do you? I've never shown you a different side of me since middle school. I gave all my time and affection into making sure you won. I helped you win. I was deeply in love with you and never received any respect or love for all that I've gave up for you, muthafucka. I settled for your choice year after year; now, it's my choice. You will either be with me, your *bestie,* and I mean for happily fucking after, and also you will neglect this past life and we will live on together as we were meant to."

"And what makes you think something so stupid like that will ever happen, bitch? I thought you were my friend, but I can't say that I didn't smell your stinking body miles away."

"Because if you don't, I'm gonna kill this pretty ass chocolate bitch in front of me. Say hey to yo man bucket." She spoke with more aggression.

Seconds later, Shanti's voice coming through the line shattered my entire heart.

"Khalifaaa! Rude, please, baby, come and get me. Bring me home please!" she yelled.

"Shanti! Shanti, are you okay, baby? Please stay calm. You know I'll find you !" I gritted my teeth as the tears built up in the corners of my eyes.

"Honest," she mumbled through the mix of her cries.

At that point, I knew it was my queen on the other side because no one understood the way we bonded if you didn't personally know us. The keyword she just spoke was the flame to get her home by any means.

"Promise," I responded, feeling those tears of rage fall.

Taki snatched the phone back and began to scream again, and I listened to every word.

"Rude Boy, you have an option now. I'm the one holding the ball, sir. I'm the one demanding the respect now, and I'm gonna be the woman you love and cherish until we both bleed in harmony."

I bit my bottom lip, placing my plan together within an instant.

"Taki, you're more than disgusting. You're a disease, someone that just destroys anything pure that's around it. I respect your request, but the only thing you will receive when I catch you is a bullet in between your fucking eyes, bitch!"

"Happy hunting, Daddy!" she giggled before hanging up in my ear.

I smashed the phone against the wall and balled my fists so tight that they were nearly about to bleed. I was about to obliterate everyone. They gave me a purpose to never show any mercy. Taki, Polar, and Lo were my new reasons. My energy was rising to kill every one of them slowly, and nothing or no team would stop me. It was time to reign reaper and king of Atlantastan.

To be continued...

Atlantastan 2:
Death To Us All

Coming Soon

Did you enjoy the read?
Let us know how much by leaving us a review on Amazon and
Goodreads.

OTHER BOOKS BY

<u>URBAN AINT DEAD</u>

Tales 4rm Da Dale

The Hottest Summer Ever

Hittin' Licks For The Holidays: Atlanta

Wet Dreams On Lockdown: The Nurse

By **Elijah R. Freeman**

Despite The Odds

By **Juhnell Morgan**

Good Girls Gone Rogue

Good Girls Gone Rouge 2

By **Manny Black**

Hittaz

Hittaz 2

Hittaz 3

Hittaz 4

Coldhearted

By **Lou Garden Price, Sr.**

Charge It To The Game

Charge It To The Game 2

A Summer To Remember With My Hitta

Snatched Up By A Hitta

Santa Sent Me A Real One For Christmas

Wet Dreams on Lockdown: The Unit Manager

Thug Me The Right Way 2

Thug Me The Right Way 3

By **Nai**

A Setup For Revenge

Wet Dreams On Lockdown: The Librarian

By **Ashley Williams**

Ridin' For You

Ridin' For You, Too

Trickin' on a Heaux for Christmas: A BBW Love Story

Homie Hoppin' For The Holidays

Wet Dreams on Lockdown: The Female C.O

By **Telia Teanna**

The State's Witness

The State's Witness 2

The State's Witness 3

This Time Won't You Save Me

By **Kyiris Ashley**

Stuck In The Trenches

Stuck In The Trenches 2

By **Huff Tha Great**

The Swipe

By **Toōla**

Melted the Heart of a Menace

Wet Dreams On Lockdown: Lieutenant Grace

By P. Wise

Merry Trapmas: Ice & Frost

By **Mia Sky**

Thug Me The Right Way

By **DiamondATL & Nai**

Wet Dreams on Lockdown: The Male C.O

By **Tamyra Griffin**

Wet Dreams On Lockdown: The Counselor

By **Paris Iman**

Wet Dreams On Lockdown: The Warden

By **Shawnice**

Wet Dreams On Lockdown: The Captain

By **TN Jones**

BOOKS BY

URBAN AINT DEAD's C.E.O
<u>Elijah R. Freeman</u>

Triggadale

Triggadale 2

Triggadale 3

Tales 4rm Da Dale

The Hottest Summer Ever

Murda Was The Case

Murda Was The Case 2

Murda Was The Case 3

Hittin' Licks For The Holidays: Atlanta

Wet Dreams On Lockdown: The Nurse